VACUUM

VACUUM

Bill James

CRÈME de la CRIME

This first world edition published 2011
in Great Britain and the USA by
Crème de la Crime, an imprint of
SEVERN HOUSE PUBLISHERS LTD of
9–15 High Street, Sutton, Surrey, England, SM1 1DF.
Trade paperback edition first published
in Great Britain and the USA 2012.

British Library Cataloguing in Publication Data

James, Bill, 1929-
  Vacuum.
  1. Harpur, Colin (Fictitious character)–Fiction. 2. Iles,
  Desmond (Fictitious character)–Fiction. 3. Police–Great
  Britain–Fiction. 4. Detective and mystery stories.
  I. Title
  823.9'14-dc22

ISBN-13: 978-1-78029-012-6 (cased)
ISBN-13: 978-1-78029-512-1 (trade paper)

All Severn House titles are printed on acid-free paper.

Severn House Publishers support The Forest Stewardship Council [FSC],
the leading international forest certification organisation. All our titles that
are printed on Greenpeace-approved FSC-certified paper carry the FSC logo.

MIX
Paper from
responsible sources
FSC® C018575

Typeset by Palimpsest Book Production Ltd.,
Falkirk, Stirlingshire, Scotland.
Printed and bound in Great Britain by
MPG Books Ltd., Bodmin, Cornwall.

ONE

Following that dreadful business when his wife and son were shot dead in the Jaguar, Mansel Shale seemed to decide on very deep changes to his own life. Evidently searching for consolation and some comfort, Shale turned to the church. Apparently, he became a regular at services and made donations beyond just the collection plate. There was talk of an endowment for a stained-glass window. Shale had a very active interest in art.

Detective Chief Superintendent Colin Harpur understood well enough how this swing to the spiritual could happen. Plenty of others before Manse had done the same when floored by grief. The possibly unique point about Shale, though, was that until this development he'd been chairman, hands-on managing director, and chief executive officer of a booming, comprehensively stocked, brilliantly profitable, recreational firm, offering its quality-guaranteed products across the entire traditional range, from Ecstasy to H. Estimates put his earnings at around £600,000–£700,000 a year, naturally untaxed, and rising very sharply in the recession.

People had less money, yes. As a result, many prioritized their spending more ruthlessly than before, went with absolute, steely dedication for the essentials. That is, they lashed out generously on stuff which would for a while blur the crisis pain and complement their Jobseeker's Allowance, although, of course, it ate into their Jobseeker's Allowance, because prices of the commodities stayed high on account of this increased demand.

Most people and most of the media thought the killings of Naomi and Laurent Shale were an error and that the real target had been Manse himself. He normally drove the Jaguar on those little routine trips, and would undoubtedly have business chums who wanted him slaughtered. It appeared someone had laid on an ambush that went wrong, possibly hiring a novice gunman. Whether or not such speculation made sense, suddenly now, Manse, ravaged by sorrow and regret, almost totally abandoned that sphere of busy commerce, as no longer morally fit for him or proper.

Of course, he might have gone either way. Some, assaulted by a tragedy of such appalling severity, would ask how God could allow it and resolve to have nothing more to do with Him. Others saw terrible events as a reminder that seeming success in the banal and basically worthless areas of life were only that – banal and worthless. They began to seek an alternative. This was Mansel's response.

He did keep the company chairmanship of his complex, but delegated all detailed running to a previous chief assistant who, Harpur's tipsters agreed, was at present definitely more or less completely clean, with a hale nasal septum and terrific dealership skills: one testimonial said he could sell pussy to a pimp. But crucially the informants also agreed he lacked command experience at rave and street level, and occasionally hallucinated about the Spanish Civil War of the mid 1930s. Some fragility was apparent in him, even conspicuous. The uncertainty sprouting from this could encourage others on the patch, or from elsewhere, to try a trade grab. The new man might look a pusher pushover, and there were plenty ready to have a go at pushing the pushover over and acquiring a rich firm.

Equilibrium had been gravely disturbed. Harpur would need to handle the fresh situation, whatever its shape and greed-powered armament. He saw the possibility of protracted, warring viciousness, conceivably a Yardie incursion. And he knew that, a rung above him, Desmond Iles, Assistant Chief Constable (Operations), thought the same.

Harpur considered that one of the most moving, temperate and surprising things about Iles was he did not altogether loathe and despise religion. In fact, he occasionally showed empathy and even a kind of hallowed enthusiasm towards the mystical. This appeared so now, in Mansel's case. Generally, Iles wouldn't have much to do with empathy or hallowed enthusiasm, except as a response to his slim-cut trouser legs and his profile, from either side. ('It would be coquettish in me to prefer one to the other,' Iles sometimes stated, and Harpur considered the case could certainly be argued.)

Yet, despite this usual prevailing focus on himself, Iles would now and then fabricate something damn close to authentic respect for others' faith and beliefs, totally regardless of what the faith and beliefs *were*: 'The complete fucking interdenominational samples book, Col,' as the ACC had once described his helpful come-one-come-all attitude in the theology compartment. He was from a Protestant Northern Irish family, but could put that aside. 'Am I going to stand between a man and his God, or, similarly, woman?' Iles said. It was the kind of question he liked – no question at all: an announcement, not requiring a damned awkward, presumptuous opinion from anyone else, thanks very much, because the only approved reply lay built-in to the tone. Although Iles possessed few tones, he screwed his money's worth from the ones he had.

But, of course, what would worry him was that Mansel's abrupt, permanent and very nearly wholesale switch to the sacred, plus transfer of the corporate management to an imperfectly rehabbed hack underling, could mean weakness; could mean, in fact, a depressingly large and perilous hole in the local mercantile power structure. Iles had helped build that structure, cherished it. 'I see myself as very like Nature itself, Col,' the ACC had said last week.

'I've heard several people state this soon after meeting you, often breathlessly, sir. Phrases such as: "That Mr Iles, though! Now, what *is* it he reminds me of? What? What? Damn it, what? Oh, I know – of course, of course: Nature!" It's not always unfavourable, I think.'

'Which people, Harpur?'

'Oh, yes, several.'

'Which aspects of Nature did they list as being apparent in myself?'

'"Nature" covers quite a variety, sir. That's one of its most famed features. Look almost anywhere and you'll find some aspect, or aspects, of Nature – larches, hillocks, and, indeed, outright hills, floods, zebras, moss, deltas, deserts, hermit crabs, west winds.'

'In what connection, as concerning myself, did they mean it?'

'These were people entitled to hold an opinion,' Harpur replied. 'British through and through, and unquestionably schooled in the fundamentals.'

Often Iles did self-scrutiny. Although others scrutinized him, he preferred his own. 'Col,' he said, 'I resemble Nature in that I abhor a vacuum. This is a well-known phrase – "Nature abhors a vacuum" – though probably not well known by you. Abhorrings wouldn't be featured in your vocab and ambit. You're glued to the Detective Chief Superintendent perch and don't have to fret about wider matters. But, look, Harpur, you unquestionably have your passable qualities, extremely valid within their limits, yes, within those limits. You are content. Myself, I have to quest intellectually – some would say reck-lessly, arrogantly, restlessly roam – in a search for mental satisfaction. That's how I am. My psychological brand. Also, however, this brings troublesome, unsparing, ruthlessly thorough insights, and I see that Shale, in his distress, has unfortunately donated us a prime, sodding vacuum.'

'Well, not exactly, sir. There has been a neat, well-schemed passing of certain powers.'

'To a nobody, Col.'

'To an established aide.'

'Established enough to be kept held down at number two until now. That is, Col, until Manse's brain and judgement had been knocked numb by tragedy and sadness, inevitably affecting his powers of choice. Haste, also, might have been involved.'

'Manse could have been grooming him for a long while. I've heard he didn't want his son in the business.'

'But please don't think I fail to see the link, Harpur,' Iles replied.

'Link? With what?'

'Myself.'

'In which respect, sir?'

'Perhaps I, too, will never in normal circumstances climb

above the second- or third-in-command spot, the *Assistant* Chief spot.' As was usual when he spoke his rank, he lingered on the 's' sounds in Assistant, like a snake hiss, to suggest enforced subservience, subordination, servility and contempt for the virulently poxed conspiracy holding him back. This was another in his limited range of tones. 'Do I, too, need some extraordinary change to the context before I can move higher? Or am I a congenital sidekick, Harpur?' Here, too, the 's' of sidekick fondled its despised s-ness.

'That is quite a bit of phrasing, sir. Not many could come up with such a combination. Almost a tongue-twister. It would definitely have stayed in my head if I'd heard folk call you a congenital sidekick.'

'Which folk?'

'Sir?'

'Which folk have you failed to hear calling me a congenital sidekick?'

'Things might continue as you want, even without Manse fully involved, sir,' Harpur replied. But he could follow the ACC's logic. This went its own simple, mighty Ilesian way, like a straight section of the Ganges in spate – speaking of Nature. He thought attempts at drugs prohibition through the law a vastly dangerous, self-defeating, blatant farce, and had for years determinedly allowed two separate, harmonious trafficking operations to function in this city: one Shale's; the other headed by Ralph W. Ember, noted environmentalist, with special concerns about urban pollution, which he raised in letters to the Press.

A major proviso to Iles's grand, permissive OK existed though. This pair had to deliver peace on the streets and preserve it: no turf fights, no drive-by salvoes to hail the New Year and/ or mark the Queen's official birthday, no domestic torchings, no body-part severances or desocketed eyes. Desocketed eyes *really* riled Iles. 'Desocketed eyes get up my nose,' he'd told Harpur a while ago. They could have no place in policy. The mind of Iles often preoccupied itself with policy. He would quote an article from a very meaty London journal, *The Economist*. Harpur had it by heart after so many repetitions, though that didn't mean he agreed: 'There is no correlation between the harshness of drugs laws and the incidence of drug-taking: citizens living under tough regimes (notably America but also Britain) take more drugs, not fewer.' Iles would say: 'Col, criminalize equals gangsterize. Only the market then controls price and distribution. Illegal syndicates maul and disembowel one another to get this control and the huge earnings that come with it – maul, disembowel, kill, maim, torture, terrorize. This is an industry producing hundreds of billions a year, Harpur. I half laugh, half mourn, when I remember all the worthy, dim efforts over the decades to achieve a "drugs-free" world. Whoever first mouthed that cheery booster must have been mainlining something prime and brain shattering. Instead, Harpur, we have a thinker as eminent as Professor Ian Gilmore, past president of the Royal College of Physicians, saying drugs should be legalized. Likewise the chairman of the Bar Council of England and Wales, Nicholas Green QC. The *British Medical Journal* states prohibiting drugs has been "counterproductive". Attempts at disruption of the trade and enforcement of anti-drugs laws are not working, a piece in *The Times* says. These are good, intelligent sources and were bound to catch up on my thinking, bless them.'

Iles maintained that possibly the greatest police objective after 'stuff the Home Office' was 'no blood on the pavement'. Throughout his domain, including drugs-pushing spots, he wanted a situation where people could walk unhurriedly and relaxed, especially younger women with brilliant arses. He, Ralph W. Ember and Manse had achieved these conditions for most of the time. Well, at least, for *some* of the time: plainly, not for Shale's wife and son. And there'd been other deaths. But, together, Manse and Ralph were strong enough to provide a reasonable degree of tranquillity under the Assistant Chief's conditional, constructive supervision. The agreement had never been explicit. Iles despised explicitness, unless, of course, he wanted something explicit. But the understanding worked. Now, with Shale's departure, Iles clearly sensed impending breakdown of the system; his careful, creative work ruined; its precise, frail, blessed balance vilely threatened. Blitzing up the Jag? A sort of blasphemy. Would the new managing director and CEO of Shale's outfit be willing to, and able to, maintain that violence-free, decently eye-socketed townscape demanded by the ACC? Would Ember agree to work with this jumped-up new boy? Also, could the amended alliance remain strong enough to smother machine pistol trouble from outside gangs trying to invade and capture some, or all, of the nicely hooked, lavish, Ember-Shale customer-base?

'Manse can't run that kind of pushing operation in his new role, sir,' Harpur had said. 'It wouldn't harmonize. The apostle James in the Bible states faith without works is dead, and probably means *good* works, not flogging skunk.'

'I direct no blame at Shale, not a fragment. Poor, desolate, endlessly suffering Manse. His present needs have to be paramount. Our requirements trail his. Tolerance, Col.' They were in Harpur's room at headquarters; Desmond Iles, wearing uniform, had called in on his way to some lunchtime civic function where he might be able to give offence. He looked snotty, brilliantly smart, would-be wholesome, evasive, utterly dandruff-clear: he looked an Assistant Chief. 'Tolerance is a quality I prize above all, except wise hate,' he said. 'In some quarters I'm known as "Forbearance Des".'

'Is that right?'

'Why shouldn't it be right, you fucker?'

'These phrases!'

'Will it last?'

'What, sir?'

'Manse Shale's "born again" experience.'

'Back to the Bible – St Paul,' Harpur replied.

'What about him?'

'In his case it went on and on, after that moment on the road to Damascus. Many an Epistle. Two each for the Corinthians, Thessalonians and Timothy.'

Iles said: 'He just wanted to bulk out the New Testament, like the long story Joyce put on the end of *Dubliners* to make a full-scale book of it.'

'That Joyce—'

'And if you say, "That Joyce – she was always a fly one," I'll kill you,' Iles replied.

In the afternoon, Harpur decided to go down to Sandicott Terrace again, where the school-run shooting had happened.

It would be his fifth trip there. Of the five, his later visits didn't have much to do with detection. There weren't any new discoveries to be made. But he'd fallen into a kind of dim ritual. It was as if he wanted to reassure himself that everything there was OK now: no further appalling incidents like those morning murders – the two people dead or dying in the Jag; the girl cowering blood-covered next to her brother's body in the back and having to be lifted out by Harpur; the demolished, low, front garden wall of a house where the car, its driver no longer a driver, got up on to the pavement at next to no speed and gave the brickwork a minor nudge . . . not enough to prompt the air bags, but sufficient to bring some destruction and stop the wheels. The wall had been repaired now.

Sandicott Terrace was a section of middling or upper suburbia, and Harpur considered it only right that a proper appearance should be quickly restored, at public expense. On the whole, he admired suburbia. It tended to be tidy. It shouldn't be subjected to turf-battle knocks. Just after the shooting, the elderly couple who lived in the property had come out on to their front lawn and spoken to Iles and Harpur. They'd rushed separately to the scene. The man said apologetically, but not apologetically enough, that he'd heard the police had lost control of the streets. His wife remarked it was as if some evil force from another way of life had taken over. Harpur recalled verbatim a few of her words: 'This is not civilization as we used to know it.' And he recalled, too, how badly that had shaken Iles. When he and Harpur were alone a bit later, the ACC said, yes, maybe some widespread evil force *was* destroying civilization and its little, sheltering walls. Harpur gave him a bit of rejoinder-bark then: 'We're a *police* force. We're here to shelter them,' he said. '*We* haven't been fucking flattened, sir.'

'Often in my prayers, Harpur, I say, "Thank you, God, for Col and his continuous, stupid optimism,"' Iles had replied.

Today, for visit five, Harpur parked a good way from the site of the shooting and walked a hundred metres or so. He stood at the minor junction where the gunman's Mondeo had waited. On the face of it, this had been an almost ridiculously simple pounce – ridiculously simple as long as the Jaguar came that way making for Bracken Collegiate private school, which the children attended. This was likely, though not totally certain. Shale's daughter had told them that he advised his wife to vary her routes there and back when she took over the run if he was away, but she would not always bother. Apparently, she didn't like to be instructed by Manse – to be bossed by Manse. So, the Mondeo had a fair chance of picking the right spot.

Harpur stood on that spot now, across the street from the restored wall. They had witness statements explaining what had happened. The Mondeo, one man in it – white, late twenties or early thirties – waited near the junction. The Jaguar came into Sandicott Terrace from the far end, the second Mrs Shale driving today, and had to slow and go round the Mondeo, aiming to turn left into the main highway – Landau Road – and on to a straight four-mile stretch to the school. But, as the Jaguar drew abreast, the automatic firing had started from the Mondeo into the Jaguar, with Mrs Shale a car's width away and Laurent, in the back, about the same. The nearness, and that kind of weapon, made it virtually impossible not to get a hit, at least of the Jaguar driver.

But the nearness also meant that if the main target should have been Mansel Shale, the gunman must have seen it was a woman at the Jaguar wheel. Nerves? No previous hit experience? Gung-ho madness – the need to kill for the sake of killing? A plan to hurt Manse, but not directly: lasting pain from immense grief? All this assumed, of course, that the objective *was* Manse, either to be eliminated himself or to be tortured by the deaths of those very close to him. Was the young girl, Matilda Shale, intended for execution, also?

The Mondeo had screamed away within a minute of the attack. Panic? Professionalism? Good luck? Exceptional luck? After all, the uncontrolled Jaguar might have taken some other streets that day. It might also have veered left not right after the shooting and hit the Mondeo, possibly disabling it.

Harpur walked back to his car. It had been another profit-less, nervous-twitch, time-wasting sojourn. He thought he had glimpsed the woman from the repaired house watching him through the front-room window. She hadn't come out to talk, though. Perhaps she could tell from his manner that he knew no more than everyone knew, and had only returned to the Terrace as a kind of face-saving spasm: his attempt to show he still governed the streets, at least until someone proved he didn't.

TWO

Naturally, others besides Iles speculated on the new situation. A couple of days ago at home Harpur's daughters had also spoken to him about Mansel Shale. Inevitably, the news of his substantial retirement from the shopping corpus had circulated. Some of the older pupils at their school, or teenagers in the clubs, had probably been customers. They'd hear of changes. The word would be around. And Harpur wondered whether one or both of the girls themselves did weed now and then and bought from Shale's people. Jill might be still a little young for that, but Hazel was fifteen. He thought he should have seen the signs, sniffed the signs, witnessed the giggles, but the girls were wily.

They found the whole Shale tale intriguing, anyway. Inevitably, the shooting of his wife and son, Laurent,[1] had made big news on television and in the papers. Shale's thirteen-year-old daughter, Matilda, who'd been in the car but survived, was Jill's age. That gave an extra interest: a sort of bond.

For much of the time, Harpur assumed – like almost everyone else – that the kills were in fact a cock-up by a hired gunman: young, cheap, incompetent, nervy, a novice. Firearms found weaknesses, in the user as well as the target, and one of the weaknesses could be wrong target. Yes, the marksman had almost certainly been sent to take out Mansel. Maybe a vengeance commission of some sort; not everyone found Shale lovable. The pot-shot briefing for this sloppy executioner must have said Manse usually drove the school-run Jaguar. Correct. So, the attack plan came down to: (a) identify the car; (b) shoot the driver, and anybody else if unavoidable; (c) scarper back to base; (d) collect the second half of the fee – in cash, not vouchers for concerts in the Albert Hall.

Mansel wasn't even aboard the Jaguar that day, though, but

---

[1] See *I Am Gold*

en route to a London conference in a different vehicle. He'd
never spoken about the shooting: or, rather, never spoken about
it to Harpur or any other officer. They'd tried to discuss it with
him, naturally, but he wouldn't have it. Simply, he quit the
active part of the game, and apparently had frequent conversations with vicars and so on these days. They'd do their best
for him, explaining considerately and patiently why life had
to be like that as part of the divine pattern: innocent people
wiped out on the way to school.

'It's what's known as *omertà*,' Jill had said. 'Crooks like
Mansel Shale don't talk to cops, even when the crooks have
been horribly hurt. *Omertà*'s Italian. I've read about it. O – m
– e – r – t – à, the "a" with an accent *grave* on it. Now, please
don't be afraid of words because they're foreign, Dad. All sorts
of them around these days owing to the European Union. Think
of Beaujolais Nouveau, which is wine, and *les sans papiers*,
which is immigrants. These Mafia racketeers sort out their own
troubles. They don't complain to the *polizia*, being the police
over there. This would stain their honour, make them finks.
They have to be *macho*. I'm glad Mansel Shale has given most
of it up. If they had another go they might kill him next time
and Matilda would be an orphan.'

'We see her some days,' Hazel said. 'She seems all right
now. She comes to judo off and on. Her dad brings her and
picks her up. The Jaguar has been repaired. He looks very
sad.'

'Well, of course,' Jill said.

'Matilda's a brave kid,' Harpur said.

'As a matter of fact, near Naples the Mafia is known as the
Camorra,' Jill replied. 'Also it's called *il Sistema*, meaning
"the system". Everything is sweetly organized, like that Brando
pic, *The Godfather*, on The Movie Channel. They have their
own lawyer, such as Robert Duvall, to state they're not breaking
the law when they're breaking the law, say through a garrot-
ting. They all believe in *omertà* and they'll kill and torture
members who go to the police, and their families.'

'What will happen now, Dad?' Hazel said. She liked to get
to the practicalities. 'There's a story around.' But she hesitated,
apparently embarrassed.

'What story?' Harpur said. He believed he could guess.

'It includes a vulgar word, Dad,' Jill said. 'But I should think you know it, in your sort of job.'

'What's that mean?' Harpur said.

'Meeting many kinds of people,' Jill said. 'Thugs, toerags, Des Iles, lowlife.'

'The story is that just before he got shot, Laurent Shale realized what was going to happen and spoke to Matilda,' Hazel said.

'Something about who had set up the attack,' Jill said, 'in his opinion.'

'Who says this?' Harpur asked, knowing he'd get a crap reply.

'I told you, Dad, it's the buzz,' Hazel said.

'Rumour,' Harpur said.

'Maybe rumour,' Hazel said.

'This word – the vulgar word – it's "twat",' Jill replied. 'Some say it to rhyme with "cat", like I have; others, especially in the United States, with "hot".'

'Yes, vulgar,' Harpur said.

'Some do say it, though, or make it a joke,' Jill said. 'For instance, there's a café called "The Warm As Toast".'

'Yes?' Harpur said. 'Yes?'

'Need the Enigma code-breaker, Dad?' Hazel said. 'The initials. We gather that what Laurent muttered just before the shooting was, "It has to be that twat Ralphy."'

'Spoken with the cat rhyme, you see, Dad,' Jill said. 'I don't know if there's research by the Oxford dictionary to show which pronunciation is top.'

'They were in the back of the car and ought to have got right down when the gunfire began, but Laurent wanted to look, so he was hit,' Hazel said. 'Matilda kept out of sight.'

Yes, that's what Laurent had said in the moment before he died, according to Matilda. She'd told Harpur just after he lifted her out of the Jaguar. She *had* quoted Laurent, using the cat rhyme. But he didn't mention any of this to his daughters.

'We think the Ralphy referred to in that sentence must be Ralph W. Ember,' Jill said. 'He's a big trader in the commodities and owns a club, The Monty. He's like you in some ways, Dad.'

'How? I don't trade or own a club,' Harpur said.

'He's got two daughters at school,' Jill said.

'Well, yes,' Harpur said. 'I think so.'

'You know it,' Jill said. 'You must have a dossier on him. But his daughters are not at John Locke Comp with us. Private: Corton House – a snob place. Ralph's rich.'

'He's known as Panicking Ralph or Panicking Ralphy,' Hazel said, 'owing to some yellowness far back.'

'It's weird, really, isn't it, Dad?' Jill said.

'What?' Harpur said.

'Ralph Ember, a crook, two kids – girls – at a private school,' Jill said. 'Mansel Shale, another crook, two kids – a boy and a girl – also at a private school, though a different one, and, of course, the boy dead now. Are crims the only ones who can afford private? Is this a hurtful question to a parent, such as you? It has to be asked, though. Is this a serious comment on the present state of things?'

'Which things?' Harpur said.

'Like the social picture in this country. Everyone hard up except the crooks,' Jill said.

'You don't want private, do you?' Harpur said.

'I'm just making a remark,' Jill said. 'Would you be able to pay if we did?'

'A hypothetical question,' Harpur replied.

'What's that mean?' Jill said. 'One you don't have to answer? There's a lot of them about.'

'Ralph Ember runs a substances firm alongside Manse Shale's, doesn't he?' Hazel said. 'And now alongside this new guy, I suppose, the heir.'

'We don't believe Laurent meant it was Panicking who actually triggered,' Jill said, 'but Laurent seemed to think Ralph had organized it, such as paying a hit man. That's what they're called in plays on the telly.'

'They both wanted monopoly, didn't they, Dad – Panicking and Manse Shale?' Hazel said. 'I've done it in Economics at school – businesses always fighting each other to destroy competition, so the winner can up prices, being the only one left with the goods. Perhaps Ralphy believes he can wipe out whoever succeeds Manse, too. Will there be more trouble? In capitalism, a company has to move forward just to stand still – referred to as a paradox, which means it's true but sounds the very opposite.'

'We discussed why exactly Laurent used the term "twat",' Jill said. 'It seemed important.'

'*If* he did,' Harpur said.

'It's someone's last statement in this life,' Jill said. 'He couldn't of prepared it, because he didn't know the shooting would happen. This word came out, like, automatic. It's his true, natural feelings. We got to give it attention. There are many hurtful words he could of selected, such as "slob" or "dickhead" or "louse", but he picked "twat". That isn't the sort of thing you'd expect to hear in a top-of-the-range Jaguar, which it was.'

'"Couldn't *have* prepared it." "Could *have* selected it." "We *have* to give it attention." None of it's certain,' Harpur said.

'People say "twat" to mean someone who's vain but not much good at anything at all,' Jill replied. 'Showy but useless. It's like "prat", only stronger. So, maybe Laurent realized it was all a mess up – his mother shot by mistake, and himself going to get it next.'

'That nickname – Panicking Ralph, or Panicking Ralphy,' Hazel said. 'It makes him sound a complete write-off, doesn't it, Dad?'

'And therefore he can be termed a "twat",' Jill said.

'All right, he might not have made a mistake with the gun himself, but because he's rubbish and drops into panics he picks the wrong man to do the job for him,' Hazel said. 'It's the kind of error football managers make when they're getting too much pressure. Bad choices.'

'Perhaps it really upset Laurent to think he was going to be killed by some jerk sent by another jerk,' Jill said. 'A sort of insult, as well as a mistake. Nothing noble about it, such as facing fearful odds in warrior sagas. And that's why Laurent used that unpleasant word.'

'A harsh protest,' Hazel said, 'but, of course, not with any evidence. It was just a guess or a feeling by Laurent.'

'We don't think Ralph Ember had any part in the shooting,' Harpur replied. 'We've talked to him.'

'And he said, "No, no, not me, guv," did he?' Hazel asked, with a villain voice. 'And you replied, "Oh, that's all right then, Ralph. Sorry, old chum. Just thought we'd ask."'

'Is he alibied?' Jill said.

'That's the kind of question Dad is never going to answer,' Hazel said.

'Who *was* behind it?' Jill said.

'We're working on this,' Harpur said.

'It's taking a time, isn't it?' Hazel said.

'These things often do,' Harpur said.

'Of course they do,' Jill said. Ultimately, she'd usually try to defend Harpur when Hazel got heavy.

THREE

The loyalty question troubled Ralph Ember's wife, Margaret. One reason it harassed her was that this shouldn't really *be* a question: she had married Ralph, had his children, and loyalty to him ought to be automatic. But, no, that was too simple. Obviously, marriages could come apart, marriages with children as much as those without. Life in the marriage could become intolerable for one or, perhaps, both spouses, and loyalty would have no place any longer.

Margaret's debate with herself wasn't to do with the usual causes of strain between husband and wife, though. Her anxieties were special. Because of the drugs business he ran, she knew Ralph might always be a target for competitors, for enemies. This was especially true now, after the Shale deaths. So, might Ralph's family be a vengeance target: herself and their two daughters? Several times during her marriage, she had suffered quite long spells of fear, but never fear as deep and unrelenting as this. It closed around her, offered not even a small sight of relief. She experienced it as a tirelessly hostile presence, standing a little back for the moment as a tease, but all the time ready to rip in.

There had been past periods when she believed the only way to rid herself of her dreads arising from Ralph's work was to take the children and leave him. She'd asked him to quit his work, and, of course, he'd refused. In fact, she had gone once,[2] but returned after only days. She often wondered later whether that had been a stupid, craven decision. She'd had the guts to up and go, but not to stay gone and settle safe elsewhere. Idiotic? Surely it was the walkout itself that required the real nerve. *Cheers then, Ralph, it's been great, but . . .*

Yet her collapse had followed. And so shamefully soon. She longed to think this frailty was deeply unlike her. She'd always

[2] See *Naked At The Window*

regarded herself as passably dogged and constant. But the memory of such jittery backtracking stuck and seemed to disable her now in this new situation, the Jaguar killings situation. She felt she might never be able to finalize a break from him. And wouldn't any second attempt to exit be . . . well, idiotic on idiotic, pathetic, no matter how scared she was of staying with Ralph – and, as a necessary part of that, making their kids stay?

This responsibility battered her. Worries about them dominated. It hadn't been quite the same during her previous quit schemes: although the children were important then, yes, she'd had other strong motives, also. But these days she had to consider the death of Laurent Shale, didn't she? Although his stepmother had been killed at the same time, it was slaughter of the boy that produced Margaret Ember's worst worries. If Shale's uninvolved kid could be wiped out, how safe were her daughters, Venetia and Fay? Vengeance could be very thorough.

Just before she did a runner from Ralph last time, she'd gone to see that slippery, crude, know-all, rough-house cop Harpur for advice. Obviously, you'd be insane to trust any police detective more than fifteen per cent with your fingers crossed – if so much – but she'd hoped he would understand her stress. He knew about murder, and not just professionally: his wife had been knifed to death in a car park.[3] And he had two schoolgirl daughters himself. Although he'd been reasonably kind and apparently straightforward then, she drew back from consulting him again now. That would be part of the idiotic, pathetic display she must avoid. *'Oh, on one of your little scoots again, Mrs Ember?'* She had to guard the tatters of what she'd come to regard as her main, shaky self.

Some things her daughters said – no, not *said*, more like hinted at – about the car shooting stoked her alarm. They had obviously gathered babble fragments from the jungle-drums, and these disturbed them. The girls nagged Margaret with vague, roundabout inquiries that seemed based on some sort of information, accurate or not, but information they dodged

[3] See *Roses, Roses*

disclosing. It was as if they blue-pencilled part of this gossip as too embarrassing or hurtful for their mother. Yet they couldn't leave it, forget it. To Margaret their badgering came across as the same question put repeatedly in changed words, like a cross-examination trick. It amounted to this: were their father and Mansel Shale violent enemies? Neither of the girls actually used the words 'violent' or 'enemies'. They went for 'business rivals', 'competitors', 'opponents'.

Struggling to unearth what they were really talking about, Margaret came to sense they might have heard suggestions that the boy, Laurent, spoke to his sister in the back of the Jaguar just before he died, said something important but perhaps crude. Margaret could not have explained how she got to this notion, but it was where her daughters' questions seemed to point, and point constantly. Perhaps he'd attempted to account for the shooting, perhaps even accused someone. If so, she could possibly guess which someone, with or without guidance from her daughters. There must be all sorts of rumour about among local kids – buzz as they called it, though the girls didn't use that word either now: they obviously aimed to keep things believable and weighty. Margaret would have liked to listen in to some of the buzz; wrong age-group, though, by decades. She, too, wanted to know whether Ralph and Manse Shale might be violent enemies. This helped explain the dazing degree of her fear. Good God, was it conceivable that Ralph commissioned some thug to rake the Jaguar, hoping to kill Shale and not caring too much about anyone else hit; had actually planned to ambush the school run?

She could see why this idea had shocked and perplexed Venetia and Fay. After all, on the face of it, at least, Ralph and Mansel Shale had been business associates, virtually pals. They'd always respected each other's interest and seemed to believe in civilized cooperation. True, they were not partners. Their companies existed independently. But they both appeared to recognize the value of a good, positive understanding between them, unofficially and lovingly backed and blessed by Assistant Chief Constable Iles. Had this understanding suddenly splintered, despite him? She'd tried to get something from Ralph about the scene, approaching the subject from what she thought of as fairly mild, general queries, the kind of questions any wife might ask any husband – if the husband dealt drugs, that is. Of course, they'd discussed the shootings and Mansel Shale's withdrawal to the chairmanship of his company.

'So there'll be someone new running Mansel's outfit,' she said. 'Will he be able to manage?'

'Manse must think so.'

'But is he in a state to gauge things right?'

'He knows his people – what they're capable of.'

'It's all happened in such a rush.'

He began to sound irritated, as if she was hounding him. 'We don't have to worry about it, Margaret, do we? It's a different company.'

'Yes, I know, but—'

'Not our concern,' Ember said. 'We mourn the deaths, certainly. Who wouldn't? Terrible, terrible. What kind of person could act like that?'

'Or hire someone to act like that.'

'Yes, or hire someone to act like that. Degenerate. But the business consequences, as distinct from the personal, are another matter, private to Manse and his people.'

'Are they, Ralph?'

'How could it be otherwise?'

She knew something like collapse of the Ralph-Shale business pact had always been possible. The soft-soap terms to describe the relationship – 'positive understanding', 'virtual pals', 'civilized cooperation', happy closeness as 'business associates' – these cheery labels would do all right for the surface, for the obvious, but *only* for the surface and obvious. What their businesses were about was what all businesses were about: the need to make and inflate profits, the need to be still here, to survive. And, in the type of businesses they ran, the survival compulsion brought persistent, very special and acute pressures. Margaret had read somewhere lately that three-quarters of entrepreneurs failed – and Ralph loved to describe himself as an entrepreneur, his central ambition to bring seller and buyer together: particularly buyers who needed regular refills for their junkiness, and who had steady raw cash, got no matter how.

That three-quarters figure applied to normal, above-board, legal businesses. For the kind of outfits controlled by Ralph and Mansel Shale this failure rate would be much, much higher, because competition was rough and ferocious, expressed often by handguns or something bigger. Had Ralph decided that Manse Shale, his dear, virtual friend, his happy business associate, his sharer of positive understanding, was, in fact, a towering menace to Ralph's own career and should be toppled? And, if so, would Shale feel he had to answer back in a similar bloody style: that is, blast a child or two on the opposing side – Ralph's side?

They said Manse was broken by sorrow and had removed himself from all routine leadership tasks in his company. As chairman, though, he could still give orders. Some would argue that chairmen existed *only* to give orders, and draw pay. Between sessions with the Litany and anthems, Mansel might have time to whisper a few harsh, tit-for-tat instructions about Ralph and his family. So, Margaret yearned to bolt in good time from the hazard area with Venetia and Fay. She believed she owed them that, though they wouldn't understand.

'I still wonder about Manse's successor,' she said.

'Wonder is OK,' Ralph said. 'Wonder is natural. But don't *worry*. Let me mention Harry Truman, US President at the end of the war.'

'Truman?' she replied. Ralph would flourish bits of knowledge now and then, like a star in the pub quiz. He had started a degree course in the local university, but suspended it for the present, to deal with what he referred to as 'exceptional counter-slump demands' on his company. There must have been some US history in Ralph's Foundation Year.

'Suddenly, Truman had to take over from Franklin Roosevelt, a brilliant President, who'd died,' he said. 'Hardly anyone had even heard of Truman. But he turned out great.'

'Do you want Shale's new man to turn out great?' she said.

'Immaterial either way.'

'Is it?'

'Totally immaterial,' Ralph replied.

'A competitor.'

'There's enough business for both the firms,' Ralph said. 'Always has been. Why should things change now?'

A kind of stifling, workaday tact and censorship had come to exist between Margaret and Ralph, and the children seemed to have adopted the style, perhaps unconsciously, possibly believing this was normal for every family and all families. Some facts were never spoken about although known to the whole household. Margaret felt partly responsible. It began, didn't it, with her attitude to Ralph's chief business? Of course, she knew this to be the drugs trade, and on a mighty scale. She'd have to be half-witted not to know. Although there was also The Monty – a drinking club he owned, cherished, and had crazy hopes for – as an earner, it didn't rate. In any case, Monty profits had to be declared for tax, meaning it rated even less. No question, the bulk of the family's income came from substances supply. She, like Ralph himself and the children, lived on this money, this gorgeously ample, freely-flowing, thoroughly-criminal wealth. The source was not discussed. Harpur's strutting, dandified boss, Iles, blind-eyed the trade, because of some special, personal theory. He treated the city as if it belonged to him and he could apply what laws he fancied, and the reverse. His attitude and behaviour did confuse the picture a little. But drug dealing remained a grave offence. Margaret knew that.

She also knew some people suffered appalling damage from drugs, including many youngsters. The Pope had spoken of the 'serpent of drug trafficking' – and sometimes the Pope got things right. She watched her daughters. Drugs could derange and destroy. Yet she and the family continued to enjoy these splendid, racketeered profits. They lived in a dignified, handsome manor house, Low Pastures, with paddocks, stables, ponies, noble chimneys, a library, and a long, curved, tree-lined drive, part gravelled, part tarmacked. Centuries ago a foreign consul had occupied Low Pastures, and, later, a Lord Lieutenant of the county. It ought to reek of wholesome distinction.

Margaret loved the property, but wasn't always at ease there. She felt like someone who would never deliberately hurt an animal but who loved *foie gras*, so made herself ignore the cruelty that produced it. The actual nature of Ralph's core business stayed unmentioned. He commandeered that gaudy term 'entrepreneur' to describe, or fail to describe, his activities. So much more elevated and vague than 'baron' – the flawed kind of baron Ralph was; much more flaw than baron. And Margaret let him sidestep like that; cowardly of her, again? The children seemed to be following. Naturally, there had been talk about the deaths of Naomi Shale and Laurent, but only general, regretful, disgusted comments; nothing potentially troublesome.

The Embers inherited a plaque fixed to one of the gates at Low Pastures by some earlier owner. Inscribed on it in elegant white lettering was *'Mens cuiusque is est quisque'* – a tag from an ancient phrase-monger, apparently. Ralph cleaned it and checked the screws for corrosion every few weeks. He didn't know any Latin, of course, but had found a couple of translations on the Internet: 'the mind of each man is the man himself' or 'a man's mind is what he is'. Not many people knew what Ralph's mind was, though. She didn't, not altogether. Ralph himself might not be totally sure. Harpur probably got as close as anyone. She reckoned Harpur had quite a mind himself, despite his job. To keep Iles from a breakout into catastrophe, anyone would need quite a mind.

'I wonder, too, what would have happened if Mansel Shale himself had been shot, as most seem to think was the real intention,' she said. They talked in the drawing room, Ralph standing alongside the long, mahogany Regency sideboard, Margaret seated on a chesterfield.

'Who seem to think the real objective was Manse?'

'It's the impression I get.'

'But where from?'

'The media coverage. General talk. And it would appear logical, don't you think, Ralph?'

'Logical how?'

'Very credible.'

'In what way?'

'Some sort of struggle for dominance, leading to the ambush.'

'You're talking Darwinism.'

'Turf rivalries.'

'Who between?'

'"The territorial imperative", as it's known.'

'That's fanciful. Who can tell what the real intention was?'

'Yes, who can, Ralph?'

He nodded, as though this was an answer, the strong, hand-some face kept empty. Many saw him as very like the young Charlton Heston. Lusting slags, especially, got wowed by the resemblance. And Margaret had an idea that some of them got more than wowed. He said: 'All sorts of hazy ideas. Bound to be. Imponderables. Ultimately, darling, such gab is useless.'

'But more or less inevitable, Ralph, surely.'

'Useless.'

She could see he might be saying only what was obvious and true. The most frequently offered explanation for the Sandicott Terrace shootings rested mainly on guesswork and theory, not definite knowledge: intelligent guesswork and theory, perhaps, but, also, as Ralph said, possibly fanciful, and ulti-mately useless. But she felt at the same time that she might have been fended off. Had she just been told in the unspoken, indirect way introduced and refined by Ralph, and accepted by her and the children, that the executions were one of those areas which could certainly be mentioned – could not be absolutely ignored – but which lay off limits as a subject for digging into and for nosy discussion? A special commercial matter best considered mostly private to Ralph?

But what made it special? She wouldn't be asking, and he wouldn't answer if she did. So, where did this leave her? It left her ignorant of the details of the Sandicott Terrace outrage and its background, and ignorant of whether Ralph knew about the details of the Sandicott Terrace outrage and its background – had, in fact, helped *create* the details and background of the Sandicott Terrace outrage.

Without telling him, she drove there. She wanted some solidity, some reality. Streets and houses would give her that. She could not remember ever having been there before, though she'd seen plenty of media photographs and films of it just after the attack. She parked about a hundred metres away and walked to the junction with Landau Road. She stood at the place where, according to the Press and TV pictures, the gunman's Mondeo must have waited. It chilled her a bit to be there. Did he have the gun on his lap as he watched in the mirror for the Jaguar's arrival? It chilled her more than a bit to think Ralph might have briefed someone to take up station there, or briefed someone to brief someone to brief someone: Ralph was cagey, probably wouldn't get too near the actuality. The buck didn't stop with Ralph, because he took care that the buck didn't reach him. She knew some people called him Panicking Ralph, or even Panicking Ralphy, which she particularly loathed. She thought 'Cautious Ralph' would suit him more exactly as a nickname. But maybe when the caution didn't work or didn't suit the situation he fell into panic.

The Jaguar driven by Mrs Shale would have slowed when it approached the junction and as it went round the Mondeo. The Terrace there was not wide. For a couple of seconds the two drivers must have been within a few metres of each other, in separate cars. Although she knew nothing about guns, this had surely been an ideal set-up for the man in the Mondeo. He'd used an automatic weapon, apparently, spraying bullets. He was bound to have a hit, or more than one.

She saw another factor in this nearness, though. At that distance, how could he have mistaken a woman for a man behind the wheel of the Jaguar – Naomi Shale instead of Mansel? But did the guesswork and theory contain the guess and theorizing that this young man with the gun was so nerve racked and inexperienced he blasted off as soon as he identified the Jaguar, incapable of narrowing his choices any further, and determined to get clear fast?

An elderly woman came out into her front garden opposite and beckoned to her. When the traffic thinned, Margaret crossed the street. 'Are you Press, that kind of thing?' the woman said. 'It's long after the event, but are you doing an atmospheric article? We've seen many journalists and broadcasting folk here. We were objects of considerable interest, owing to proximity. Most likely you'll note our wall has a new section. The Jaguar knocked a hole, you see. It's possible to find symbolism in that.'

'I wanted to see the actual site,' Margaret said.

'Not Press? General interest?'

'That kind of thing.'

'Crime, violent deaths fascinate some. I do not object. Tastes are personal. Or are you connected with one or more of the parties concerned? If it's one of those killed, you have my sympathy. Obviously. We get one of the detectives down here gazing about as if he thinks clues will come floating by on the wind even now, days and days after. Maybe he wants to reassure us by his presence that they're still on the case. Yes, still on the case and getting nowhere. This is not the top man himself, Iles, but his dogsbody, Harpur. Their names have been in the media a lot, of course. Our view – my husband's and, to an extent, mine – is they've lost the fight for control of the streets. There's no safety, no lasting tranquillity. It looks like he – that's the Harpur one – comes here to demonstrate he hasn't given up or handed over, pacing about and looking thoughtful. Oh, splendid, when nothing much is happening here, as is the usual. Well, excellent. But what about gunfire and a child and a woman destroyed? That's a different item, wouldn't you say?

'We long for the kind of civilization we used to have. As a society we're on the slide. Mrs Thatcher, as she was then, thought society didn't exist. It does, but it's breaking down. Whose fault is that? I'm not talking behind their backs. I told them the same on the day. That Iles, poncing about like a Nureyev. And now this government coalition, as it's known, is going to cut the number of officers. Economies. Consider this – would our wall have been repaired under the coming regime of penny-pinching? I look at these new bricks and recall they were made necessary by an off-course car with two corpses aboard, for reasons unknown. Unknown to us, anyway. This is not a cheerful idea. Would you care to come in for a cup of tea with hubby and me? The house is quite safe pro tem.'

FOUR

Luckily, Denise always slept very heavily, especially after she and Harpur had made love, and he was able to leave the bed at just before three a.m. without seriously disturbing her. As he moved, she did porker-snort mildly twice, eyes still shut, and reached out with her right hand as if to get her ciggies and lighter from the bedside table. Harpur pushed them nearer her. This seemed only humane. And, in any case, it always thrilled him to see her take a first fiercely comprehensive, feverish pull at the charred nicotine with lips that looked made for it. The charge of smoke went for sure right down deep and pervasive in her, a homely place to be.

Naturally, a portion of it would come back out and drift close around her ears, like buttonholing her to confide something. Harpur considered Denise the kind to be worth confiding things to, quite a few things. But there was no real commitment and determination in her blind search for the twenty-pack this morning: not much more than a subconscious, tobacco-programmed twitch. She turned on to her stomach, jabbed her hand back under the duvet as though it had culpably been AWOL and resumed full, reasonably quiet blotto-ness, which she excelled at. Harpur had dozed only, knowing he must be away so early for the break-of-day raid. He'd set the alarm for seven thirty so Denise could get the children's breakfast and see them off to school.

It delighted Hazel and Jill when Denise was around to do breakfast, not just because of the full-fat meal. After all, Harpur and the girls themselves at a pinch could cook breakfasts. But they considered that for her to be there in a dressing gown first thing made for something like a family occasion. Denise wasn't really family, absolutely wasn't family, though she and Harpur had been sort of together off and on for a while. Now and then in her university term time she would stay the night at her room in the Jonson Court student block. More often, she slept here with Harpur, and the children thought this great. They considered it helped repair things.

Denise permanently left in Harpur's wardrobe the short blue dressing gown and old pair of suede desert boots she wore here at breakfast, and they took this as a sign she belonged. A while ago, their mother, Harpur's wife, Megan, had been knife murdered in the station car park after a late journey back from London by train, and they were bound to miss her still. For them, Denise brought some of that old, comforting completeness. Like Megan, Denise was something of an intellectual, but fitted in as natural to the household.

Harpur had the idea she didn't greatly enjoy this. She wouldn't want to be regarded as a replacement mother. Of course not: she was an undergraduate at the university up the road, still less than twenty, only a few years older than Hazel. But Denise, although so young, had the mature decency and kindness to hide her objections from the kids. She obviously saw they needed consolation and felt compelled to give it. Denise could be very dutiful.

Occasionally, Harpur would try to talk to her about marriage, about actually becoming family, really cementing that completeness, making the completeness complete, the belonging secured by more than a dressing gown and stained boots. He would have loved this, and so would the girls. He'd worked out where they'd have the reception: not Ralph Ember's club. He sensed Denise didn't go for the marriage idea, though. He could understand. Dutifulness didn't reach that far. Harpur was nearly twice her age. Hazel and Jill called his taste in music, clothes and hairstyles unforgivable, even for someone in the police. He thought she spent some nights in her student bed to underline that it had not become a settled, shacked-up arrangement with him. This hurt.

As to clothes, Harpur dressed as quickly as he could now in the dark. He put on what he regarded as a pretty good Marks and Spencer, double-breasted, dark-grey suit; a white shirt; tasteful blue and silver tie; and black, high-price, lace-up shoes. Some said you could spot police detectives by their expensive shoes. If you were going to trample through someone else's noble property, as he probably must this morning, you needed to have something fine on your feet. In fact, the kind of 'open-up-it's-a-raid' call he would be on soon demanded a respectable and respectful appearance generally, not just shoes. He thought Denise had probably never seen him so radiantly togged out. She might be impressed, even persuaded into a rethink about something established and permanent with him, such a bandbox. But, no, she wouldn't be. She wasn't one to be wowed by tailoring or lace-ups. Her mind took her elsewhere.

One of the problems was that Denise had told him she'd been listening lately in her Jonson Court room to a recorded book called *Fear of Flying*, which caused a small storm apparently when it came out as a volume in the 1970s. It had been issued lately on CD, and Denise thought its message very sound. She said the story's heroine sought and recommended what she called the 'zipless fuck', meaning a sex session free from commitments or significance beyond itself. The heroine travelled in her quest for this. 'As Gertrude Stein might have said, Col, a fuck is a fuck is a fuck,' she'd told Harpur.

'Gert always got to the nub,' Harpur replied.

Denise did a lot of reading, or being read to, not just about categories of shag. Some works she'd discuss with Harpur, who appreciated these slices of education from her. They might help him catch up. She had a French poem where the writer moaned he had come too late into a world that was too old. Harpur sometimes felt like this, though he realized that if he had come into the world earlier he'd be even older now.

Because of Denise, he knew her accommodation building was named after a big English literary figure who had no 'h' in Jonson; but there was another famous Johnson who did. Only the ignorant mixed them up. Harpur didn't think he'd ever mix them up because he wouldn't be referring to either. Also, he'd discovered from Denise that the name of the German writer Goethe was not pronounced like the Biblical 'goeth', but to rhyme with frankfurter. However, Harpur found her comments on *Fear of Flying* troublesome. She prized the book, and would sometimes beat off Harpur's talk of a wedding by praising this happy ziplessness. 'It was written around two decades before I was born—'

'Not from a zipless fuck.'

'—and conditions for women have changed, yes, but its argument is still interesting,' she'd said.

'Doesn't she mean a single zipless fuck between people who don't know each other and will never meet again?' Harpur had argued. 'One-night stand. Whereas, we've had a lot of fucks and will probably continue to have a lot as long as my back's OK and so on. Are they *all* zipless?'

'What "and so on"?' she replied. 'You never mentioned an "and so on" before. This is the trouble with older men.'

'Which other older men have you known?'

'And they're liable to jealousy.'

'The children think *you're* liable to jealousy.'

'Who of?'

'You've got a point there,' Harpur replied.

'In any case, Erica Jong, the book's author, didn't *invent* the zipless fuck.'

'Had it been patented by someone else?' Harpur said.

'An American woman poet, 1920s, tells a lover that, though she's enjoying a screw with him for now – for *now*, only – he needn't imagine she'll want to talk to him tomorrow.'

'Are you scared of conversation then?'

'Some topics are OK.'

'Which?'

'Many.'

'Which?'

'Oh, yes, some are OK.'

And Harpur always had to leave it at that. He realized that among other factors she might be thinking of her parents in Stafford. They probably wouldn't feel ecstatic if she announced she was going into something permanent and definitely zipped with a widower not far off forty, plus his two gabby, managing teenage daughters. This wasn't what Mr and Mrs Prior had in mind when they coughed up all that money on fees and maintenance for a degree course and sent her off. Praise be for mobile phones: her parents needn't know how infrequently she overnighted in Jonson Court, without an 'h', and without that capitalized 'H', Harpur.

He kissed her on the back of her neck, as farewell, all that was available for kissing, except her hair. She grunted into the pillow, and he took it as a meaningful grunt, not just piglike now, and with his name specifically on it; as affectionate and personal as could be expected at three a.m. But what a tragedy she couldn't see him in his sterling, dawn-caller gear.

He wanted to believe, and did half believe, they'd got beyond the zipless. He thought she knew this, but didn't like admitting it: an ego thing, an ageist thing. Damn powerful, disastrously powerful – the ageist thing. There'd be a lot of men as young as herself living in Jonson Court who kept up to attractive scratch on music, hairstyles and clothes. Being undergraduates, they'd probably know about the proper rhyme for Goethe, and wouldn't have to waste time discussing it. Did she listen to that book CD alone? Harpur was bound to wonder whether any zipless fucks took place in her room.

At the university, she did what to Harpur seemed a strange mixture of 'modules', as courses were called: some literature, some languages, some engineering and engineering drawing. 'Got to be all-round,' she'd said. 'What employers want. Tough days. Graduates have to tailor themselves.' He'd suggested that having mastered these subjects she'd be able to design a new tram for steep French streets and tell the passengers in their own lingo about the poet who considered the world too old.

When he was half way down the stairs Jill, in pyjamas, came out from her bedroom. She switched on the landing light and said: 'Dad, you're looking rather pathetically naff in that outfit.'

'It's necessary.'

'Is this for a small hours, battering-ram hit on some poor sleeping suspect, Dad?'

'Why aren't *you* asleep?' he replied.

'I was. I heard movement.'

'But I was silent.'

'I'm tuned in, even when asleep. It's part of my . . . my, like . . . part of my very *being*. That's the trouble with lace-ups: I can hear them being tied. Do people of your big rank usually go on cockcrow busts?'

'It's not a bust.'

'It *is* nearly cockcrow, though.'

'A special operation.'

'To do with the Mrs Shale and Laurent murders?'

'Special.'

'Will Mr Iles be there?'

'It's part of a wide pattern of inquiries,' Harpur said.

'The four thirty a.m. bang on the door. I read people are supposed to be really, like, low in theirselves then.'

'So you should go back to bed. And it's "really low in *them*selves", no need for "like".'

She'd been speaking to Harpur from alongside her bedroom door. Now, she shifted slightly and seemed about to come part way down the stairs to where he stood. She'd want to give him a close once-over to see if she could make out a full shoulder holster shape under his coat, and possibly a flak jacket.

'No,' he said. 'Sleep again now.'

'Is it dangerous?'

'It's a call. We'll have plenty of people there.'

'Mr Iles? Is it his idea? If it's his idea, it *could* be dangerous. He goes looking for risks because he's sure he'll win, or because he's not sure he'll win, but wants people to think he *is* sure he'll win, so he'll look strong and Ilesy, and because he gets so bored with ordinary police stuff, especially now he's stopped chasing Hazel because he knows she's got a steady boyfriend[4]. He wants something to get his blood going.'

'Denise will do you black pudding,' he replied.

'Oh, Dad, life isn't just about breakfasts, you know.'

He recognized there were times when he disappointed her. She thought he trivialized and dodged, whereas she tried for a more cosmic approach to things, a bit like the ACC.

She gave up the plan to get nearer now and shifted towards her bedroom. He didn't say anything else in case it started her bloody well quizzing and misty psychologizing again. He glanced back up as he went from the house, and she'd disappeared, her door closed. He drove out to the rendezvous point not far from Ralph Ember's house and spread, Low Pastures.

---

[4] See *Girls* and previous titles

Jill's theory about sleep patterns might not apply to Ralph. His club, The Monty, in Shield Terrace, closed at two a.m., and Harpur knew Ember generally went there just before, to make sure everything was properly locked up and to put the takings in the safe or drive them to the bank's twenty-four-hour drop-off. By the time he reached home again it would be close to three a.m., so he might only have been in bed an hour and a bit when the police party arrived.

Iles rang the bell himself. The house was dark. Ember opened up almost immediately. He had his day clothes on, shoes and all.

'Ralph, here's a treat!' Iles said.

'I heard you'd be showing here at around this time today,' Ember said.

'Heard from where?' Harpur said.

'What's it about, Mr Iles?' Ember replied.

'Harpur has a warrant. He's first class at that kind of rudimentary admin thing. And he dresses up for it, in his funny little way. I've got pals accompanying me here, Ralph, who'll go through your property with total, unremitting delicacy, making their necessary and thorough searches, yes, but not at all in disruptive style. And utter decorousness will be maintained when it comes to your sleeping family, all female, in, obviously, their respective beds.

'You may have heard the police phrase, to "spin a crook's drum", meaning brutally and hunnishly to ransack a suspect's living quarters seeking evidence. This would hardly be the method adopted in a visit to the distinguished *gentilhommière* Low Pastures, would it, Ralph? We're glad the plaque on your gates is being kept in good nick. "*Mens cuiusque is est quisque*." Good old Cicero! He loved a bit of wordplay. "Get your hook into a man's mind and you can land the man himself." Makes things sound so damn easy, doesn't it? But I wonder. How's *your* mind these days and nights, Ralph?'

'What's all this about, Mr Iles?'

'That's the point I'm making,' Iles said.

'Well, yes, but what's it about?' Ralph replied.

'What's it about? An entirely fair question,' Iles said.

'Obviously, it's not a mere social call – not so early, and with all these people.'

'So what's it about?' Ember said.

Iles could obviously have answered, but didn't. The idea for the raid hadn't come from him. Jill was wrong on that, too. A week ago the Chief himself had called Iles, Harpur, Francis Garland and a couple of trained property-search detectives to a meeting in his suite. The Chief put on a series of first-class, almost triumphant, smiles, and looked resolved and positive. 'The Shale-Ember situation – I see it as an opportunity,' he said. 'A considerable exploitable plus. This should be our constant aim, to transform what might be regarded as a setback – in this case, the double murder – into an asset. We've watched one half of the substances trade take an enormous hammering with the fall of Mansel Shale. We sympathize with him, to some extent, of course we do, even though he has chosen the type of career where that kind of thing – the Jaguar ambush kind of thing – can happen. But we also view his removal as an opening, a brilliant invitation. Now we must smash the other half of the crooked confederation, and smash it while a degree of shock and chaos affects the scene. If we are decisive, quick and thoroughly crash-ball in method, we could come out of this with a uniquely drugs-free city.'

Had the Chief ever heard Iles slag off the campaign for a drugs-free world? Was this a deliberate send-up of the ACC? Would the Chief risk that? Maybe. Iles had been able to control, and finally destroy, a previous Chief Constable, Mark Lane, through cheek, contempt, taunts and a faster brain. He used to call Lane's wife 'the power behind the clone'. So far, though, Iles hadn't even got close to squashing Sir Matthew Upton, Lane's replacement.

'And the alternative?' the Chief had said. 'There are two possibilities. One – the most likely, in my view – is that Ember expands his business to colonize what used to be Shale's operation. This must have been a temptation and aim even before the shooting. Ember's formidably strong now, but he would be stronger still. No doubt he already sells to prominent media people, Chamber of Commerce people, Round Table, educational and political people, who can put in a word for him when there are problems. Don't tell me that university vice-chancellor lady I've met at functions now and then got so intermittently bold without sniffing something quality maintained and free from over-mix. Ralph's list of such powerful mates might double. He'd become virtually unassailable. We couldn't move against him without endangering the whole social fabric.

'The GB social fabric is already flimsy. Consider the fan club that's emerged for the killer Raoul Moat. He's their hero. People are not necessarily on our side. I hope everyone understands the significance of Moat and his admirers. Consider also the middle-class anarchists with their stated objective to shaft the police in the student fees riot in London.

'The second potential development is that new, suddenly aspirational, minor local pushers, or firms of any size at all from outside our ground, will spot the gap left by Shale and aim to fill it. There's been plenty of publicity about the situation here. It will sound like an invitation to villains everywhere. Nature abhors a vacuum. We could very soon have a territorial war on our hands, perhaps involving Ember, perhaps featuring other gangs, based here or not.'

A second echo: maybe in the Chief's hearing Iles had spoken one day about his emphatic agreement with Nature in the vacuums matter. Was Upton calculatedly echoing some of Iles's themes, ridiculing him, toying with him? Did the Chief really have that kind of arrant fearlessness and lunacy?

'The logic of this, it seems to me, is that we should as a first-stage operation achieve the removal of Ember,' Upton had said. 'Alone, Ralphy and his outfit are comparatively easy meat.' He smiled, and his voice became the gentle voice of gorgeous reasonableness. 'Now, I hope I'm not an as it were serf to logic and the cerebral. I know there are other considerations, other impulses. Some of these at their proper time may be wholly valid. We are not all mind and deduction. Gut-feelings about a situation do often count, and we all have some of those, and are the better for it. But logic, when it is insistent and indisputable, must surely be allowed ultimately to guide, to predominate. Current developments present us with a splendid chance to dispose of the Ember interests as first phase of a comprehensive purging. In that first phase, he and his dealership will be obliterated.' Now, the Chief had become terse and commanding. 'I want you to arrange an immediate, full-out strike against him, Desmond, Colin.'

'In what form, sir?' Iles said.

'This would be a completely justified move,' Upton said. 'I regard Ember as, first, a leading suspect as organizer of the Naomi and Laurent Shale murders, and second, a flagrantly major drugs purveyor, with that grog-shop, The Monty, and his ponderous letters to the Press on environmental topics, a cover. It is a cover we shall no longer be fooled by.'

'I was intrigued by a phrase you used, sir,' Iles replied. 'I took a note.'

'Which?'

Iles made as though to read from a pad. 'About Nature abhorring a vacuum.'

'Something of a cliché, I fear, Desmond. Not at all original.'

'Nonetheless, sir, it is *your* cliché. You have corralled it, enlisted it under your, as it were, ensign. There are many clichés out there, clamouring for an inclusion in serious discourse, a whole bucketful of trite folk wisdom, but this is the one – Nature, vacuums – this is the one you selected, you as a Chief. I would suggest this gives it special status, extraordinary impact.'

'In a sense, yes,' Upton said.

'Why that particular cliché was chosen is, perhaps, some-thing all of us in this room can learn from,' Iles said.

So, Upton hadn't got the phrase from Iles, had he? Or were these two at some subtle, injurious game, both pretending this was the first time Nature and a vacuum had cropped up between them? Why would they do that? Harpur couldn't have said. But, then, he very often failed to work out Iles's motives and tactics. And perhaps Upton, too, knew how to disguise his.

Harpur did spot that the ACC must have decided it was about time to start torching Sir Matt's silver-leaf grandeur. Iles's words just now were mild, but blatantly piss-taking. The others in the room had clearly noticed this, also. Francis

Garland and the two search officers looked deeply relieved. They exulted. The true, traditional Iles was once again on show – viciously polite, ruthless, ungovernable, for quite lengthy stretches more or less sane. Normality – Iles's – was struggling to re-establish itself, like morale in a beaten army. For months, all the Force must have felt uneasy that he appeared pasteurized, neutered, under a new Chief. As one of its opening ploys, the current Upton regime seemed to have reduced and squeezed Iles into his restricted role as an Assistant Chief, and *only* an Assistant Chief. Or, as he would hiss-spit it, Assis . . . ssstant Chief. This would disturb people. It suggested life had become gravely unbalanced: that the organization here had developed a perilous tilt because Iles no longer supplied his time-tested, malign, stabilizing ballast.

But these anxieties could be buried now. He'd returned with a splendid array of fresh, poisonous trickery. He had begun to restore some of his patiently, meticulously crafted discord. Because of him, the local police scene suddenly reverted. It grew recognizable and coherent. It would conform to the beloved, awkward, pre-Sir Matt mishmash pattern. Did Upton realize what was happening, the poor, articulate, benighted, beknighted sod?

'That is a phrase with scope, sir,' Iles had said. '"Nature abhors a vacuum."'

'Well, certainly,' Upton said. 'Why it has survived, I expect.'

'Timelessly useful,' Iles said. 'Nature's not one of your here-today-gone-fishing-at-the-weekend items.'

Upton said: 'But perhaps we shouldn't get too preoccupied with a form of words. I want to consider how we—'

'If we analyse that phrase, "Nature abhors a vacuum", we come up with some fascinating results, I believe,' Iles replied, joyfully steamrollering the Chief.

'Yes, unquestionably,' Upton said, 'but—'

'Not only fascinating in an academic, seminar sense, where ideas are kicked about for the very pleasure of kicking them about – to no practical purpose,' Iles said. 'We, it can be reasonably stated, are concerned with the *application* of these ideas.'

'Indeed, yes,' Upton said.

'It's why analysis of this particular idea is worthwhile, in my view,' Iles said.

Upton said: 'Yes, yes, but—'

'I think that in the phrase "Nature abhors a vacuum", Nature is put forward as something good, something lofty, impeccable, something inherently right, something setting fine standards. This is Nature in the Wordsworthian sense – Nature as a supreme, benign, godlike entity. Not Nature as in the unpleasant, dark phrase "Nature red in tooth and claw".'

'Absolutely,' Upton said.

'Good,' Iles said. 'And if I were to ask my four colleagues here, I'm sure they would agree, too. Is that not so, Col?'

'Nature is quite a massive notion, true,' Harpur replied. 'Many's the time I've become aware of that – just look at the Atlantic, or lice infestation, or Lord Heseltine's arboretum.'

Iles began to tremble a little, producing a strobe effect from the silver buttons of his uniform. A fleck of saliva dropped to the table. It shone weakly there under the lights like a poor imitation diamond. Harpur, of course, recognized these signs, and he thought Francis Garland would, too. Harpur dredged hard in his brain for a distraction.

Iles talked direct to Upton. 'Although new to this region, sir, you've probably got on the tom-toms that both Harpur and Garland here were banging my wife not so long ago, though at different times. Oh, definitely not during the same months. This I can assure you of. That would have been seedy, a simultaneous turn-and-turn-about arrangement. There was no what one might call overlap. But they will most probably have a different definition of "Nature" from the one you and I hold. They would consider they were only reacting to irresistible, endemic dong prompts from Nature when giving one on the quiet to a very senior officer's wife. I don't think, however, we need to follow them in that perverse and perverted reading of the term "Nature".'

Upton said: 'Desmond, please, these are concerns that you, you only—'

'You'll naturally wonder, sir, where this kind of activity took place. I have to tell you: certain known flophouses, public parks, cars, including police vehicles, and—'

'"Nature" figures in many a tag,' Harpur said, 'such as "force of Nature" and "laws of Nature".'

Iles abruptly came out of the flashback cuckold-fit, as was his style when forcefully interrupted – like someone emerging from a *petit mal* episode. 'And then "abhors",' he said. 'This is a mightily powerful word – beyond "hates" or "loathes" or "despises".'

'That's so,' Upton said.

'Now, if we have something as good as Nature *abhorring* at full pitch a vacuum it must mean, mustn't it, that there is nothing worse than a vacuum, or else Nature, a generally uncarping, even generous, old biddy, would not find it abhorrent?'

'That might be a fair inference,' Upton said.

Iles jumped: 'Therefore, we must all agree, mustn't we, that if drugs firms occupy that vacuum – thus, in fact, putting an end to the vacuum by their presence – this must be better than an absence of drugs firms, for such an absence will result in a vacuum, won't it? That was the kind of commendable situation – the tenanted vacuum – yes, the kind of commendable situation we had while Manse Shale ran his business. Perhaps it will resume under Shale's successor.'

'But I wish to fill that vacuum by other means, Desmond,' Upton had said from his head-of-the-table place, in a sweetly level, fuck-off-you-fartarsing-verbalizing-fool kind of tone.

'With what, sir?' Iles said.

'With what in what sense?' Upton replied.

'"Fill that vacuum" with what?' Iles said. 'People selling sarsaparilla? Or giving out Bible tracts? Or recruiting youth for the war in Afghanistan? There will always be drugs, sir. It is better that the dealing should be confined within an area – the notional vacuum area, as it were – and expertly supervised by fine, though freewheeling, grossly libidinous, folk like Harpur here and Garland. Plus, of course, the Drugs Squad.'

'You think Shale's successor in the firm will bring stability?' Upton said. He consulted a note. 'Michael Redvers Arlington? You consider he can maintain peace and order? This is someone, as I've been told, Desmond, who from time to time

believes he is the late General Franco and, wearing a tricorne
hat bought from some military uniform shop, gets on the phone
to today's German Defence Ministry to request the bombing
of the Basque town Guernica by Field Marshal Goering's
aircraft. "It's General Franco calling." I gather he can't speak
German or Spanish, so compromises with English. Delusions
of grandeur would hint at schizophrenia or bipolar disorder.

'As far as we know, he isn't addicted to anything at present,
so these mental troubles start from deep within, are integral,
not merely prompted by come-and-go outside influences – say,
H or crack. Perhaps the name of that road here, Valencia
Esplanade, planted the Spanish idea in him, and it has stuck.
Megalomania? Oh, I recognize that Bertrand Russell said
although most lunatics suffered from this, many great men in
history did, too. Maybe that's the bet Shale is making. And
you, also, think Arlington is one of the great men of the future,
do you, not a part-time madman?'

Iles said: 'Well, sir, we all have our little spells of—'

'I hear he vows to throw his enemies over a cliff to avenge
the Rightists killed like that at Ronda in the Spanish Civil War,
at least according to Hemingway in *For Whom the Bell Tolls*.'

Iles said: 'I suppose we're all inclined to say things when
excited that—'

'But Arlington and the ruins of Mansel Shale's firm are not
my principal concerns at present,' Upton said. 'I want the
elimination of Ember as a trade master. Our two Enter-and-
Search Officers with us today will give a survey now of the
Low Pastures interior and the outbuildings. They will, of
course, accompany you on any visit you make to Ember's
property.'

After their excitement at seeing Iles get back to being Iles,
the pair of officers had slumped a bit in boredom when he
went on about his wife and the parks, etcetera. Most headquarters staff had frequently witnessed and heard this kind of
outburst from the ACC. Some enjoyed every further performance; others did not. Anyway, now the two perked up and on
a conference easel showed flip-chart plans of the manor house
and sketches of its grounds, stables and gardens.

'Essential, as ever, in this kind of project that the search is swift,' Upton said, 'so that no destruction or concealment of evidence might be effected. But I hardly need to say this to people of your experience, Desmond, Colin, Francis.'

Iles said: 'Ralph Ember is—'

'I read in *The Times* that Stephenson, head of the Met, talking to the Police Foundation, estimates that only just over a tenth of the most prosperous organized criminal gangs in Britain are effectively countered by police,' Upton replied. 'Six hundred and sixty out of six thousand. I want us to be one of that six hundred and sixty. I want us to be in that tenth, and near the top of it, or actually first, Desmond, and I wouldn't say we are at present. Would you?'

Iles said: 'With someone like Ember we—'

'Would you claim we are in that tenth, Desmond?' Upton had asked.

Iles said: 'What we have to remember with someone like Ralph Ember is—'

'I certainly shall not presume to enter into the details of how this operation is to be conducted,' Upton said. 'But I thought it only wise and helpful to order up these drawings for our meeting today.'

In the lift, Iles said: 'Col, this one isn't a cunt, not like that cunt Mark Lane.'

The ACC prepared the Ember visit over the next few days. Now, as the team entered Low Pastures, he said: 'Chief Inspector Francis Garland is in charge of this little excursion, Ralph. He is Gold command. Harpur and I are here as observers only. We considered someone of your standing required our attendance. Garland has his unsavoury side, but that shouldn't affect things now.'

'What are you looking for?' Ember said.

'Well, I'm glad you were here to open up for us,' Iles replied. 'This is a true, stout front door, as one would expect in a property of such character.' He fingered it respectfully. 'Wood at its most genuine and formidable, fashioned to keep out rabble and rioters, not some three-ply, curling-at-the-edges job. I don't think our bold battering-ram would get anywhere, trying to knock this door flat, but we did bring it, just in case.'

'If I knew what you're looking for I might be able to help you,' Ember said.

'You've always tried to make things easier for us, Ralph,' Iles said. 'Don't think that's unrecognized, though some – some with power – misunderstand you.' He sighed at the absurdity of this attitude, plus its cruelty at not recognizing Ralph's virtues. 'There are a few who regard R.W. Ember as a sliver of criminal shit. Nothing that I say can move them from this view, and, as you would expect of me, I speak plenty in your favour, with many references to your accomplishments – verifiable references.'

'Oh God,' Ember replied.

FIVE

Margaret Ember would normally half wake up when Ralph returned from his club at around three thirty a.m. and joined her in bed. Now, though, she came to with 4.16 on the illuminated night clock. Ralph was not beside her. At once she made herself fully alert and listened. She could hear no movement in the house. Perhaps he'd been delayed. Occasionally, that would happen. Special celebration parties for, say, a christening, or bail, might carry on past the usual two a.m. shutdown. Ralph could be flexible. He believed in social duty, and social obligations, even to the kind of society that used The Monty. Although he wanted to make the club different – classier, and, yes, distinguished – until it *was* classier, even distinguished, he would dutifully act as the host of how it was at present.

But his absence now fretted her, merged into that general uneasiness about the trade scene since Sandicott Terrace. On top of this, she'd always worried because Ralph loaded himself with the day's takings and carried these alone to the club safe upstairs, or motored them to the out-of-hours bank strongbox. It was only a short trip, though long enough and well-known enough for trouble. She could still worry about Ralph as Ralph, not merely as someone who commanded a gang, and who might bring distress on the children and herself. He was her husband, had been her lover. From certain angles he did look gloriously like the young Charlton Heston, and she still felt tenderness for him, despite the sections of his life and thinking deliberately walled off from her. She believed that whatever he did or thought in those unreachable areas they would be intended for the benefit of her, Venetia and Fay.

But, of course, he might get that wrong, get it absolutely upside down: he could be delivering them into obvious major risk. She was aware of a customary, harsh dilemma swiftly taking her over again as she lay there seeking sleep: should she stick with Ralph because he loved them, wanted to protect them, brilliantly provide for them? Or should she and the girls put distance between themselves and him because he couldn't help exposing them to big peril? He was Ralph Ember, business associate and possible competitor of Mansel Shale in the snort, smoke and needle vocation. Shale had apparently been selected for wipeout. It looked as though things went wrong and his wife and child took the bullets instead. This disaster could produce a lot of resentment and call for at least matching revenge; possibly, enhanced revenge. Honour might be involved: Sicily didn't have a monopoly on vendettas. She knew some would regard the calamitously messed-up execution as typical of almost any operation Ralph tried to run. That would not cause enemies to go any easier with him and his, though. She wanted her daughters unhurt, alive.

Because segments of Ralph's history, and of his present, remained hidden from her, she couldn't tell whether the contempt for him held by some was fair – held by some males only: women warmed and swarmed to him. But Margaret didn't want to be linked to an incompetent, a fool. Of course, everyone knew he had his absurd dreams for The Monty. She could put up with those. He believed, or pretended to, that given time he could turn the Shield Terrace haunt into something like one of those super-respectable London clubs, say the Athenaeum or Boodle's.

He seemed greatly to like the Boodle's idea because of the craziness of the name, and the fact that Churchill once belonged: this was the calibre of membership he would insist on for The Monty in its new form. Ralph had told her he wouldn't take the Boodle's title for his relaunched club – would probably be prevented by law from doing that – but he would aim for a pleasant, Boodle's type atmosphere, except he'd let women in, which Boodle's didn't. His hopes were mad. But almost everybody cherished some impossible yearnings. They could help keep one hopeful and active. Kid boxers aimed to be Ali; male golfers would like to be Woods, especially on account of the girls. Recently, Margaret came across a saying by the famous American writer Mark Twain: 'Don't part with your illusions. When they are gone you may still

exist, but you have ceased to live.' Probably, Ralph knew how
ridiculous his fancies for The Monty were, but he needed a
grail to keep him positive. Nobody despised him for this kind
of bonkers reverie. He'd look deeply and truly idiotic, though,
if associated with a disastrous fault in the targeting of Manse
Shale, and possibly other workaday faults, concealed from her.
God, Ralph, how and when did you get to be such a mess?

Someone rang the front doorbell. It was a strong, urgent
kind of ring. She thought: 'Hell, something's happened to dear
Ralph. They've come to tell me face-to-face. Oh, Christ, how,
but how, could I have planned to ditch Ben Hur?' She swung
out of bed, grabbed her dressing gown, and opened the door
on her way to answer. But then she heard what she recognized
as Ralph's footsteps, shoed, moving swiftly in response across
the flagstoned hall. He glanced up to where she stood on the
landing and with his hand spread gave a little wave. She took
it to mean she shouldn't panic: things were OK, and he'd see
to any caller. She was terrified.

He seemed to have expected the visit; it must be why he
wasn't in bed. She tried a big whisper that she hoped would
carry: 'Ralph, don't open the door. Who's out there at this
hour? Is this part of it?' No time to define the 'it'. She wasn't
supposed to know much about the 'it', anyway – it being the
Sandicott murder spree. Was he armed?

He waved again, signalling: *Relax, dear! El Cid can cope*,
though he didn't actually say anything. His walk became almost
a swagger. He opened up, no hesitation, no squint through the
judas hole.

And no gunfire, thank God. She heard someone exclaim
faux-fondly: 'Ralph, here's a treat!' No, not just someone: she
thought she recognized the voice of that insolent, egomaniac,
eternally mystifying cop Assistant Chief Iles.

Ralph said: 'I heard you'd be showing here at around this
time today.' And then there was another voice, apparently
coming from behind Iles. She couldn't make out these words.
Iles began to speak in a foul, smarmy tone about the quality
of the front-door wood and about searching Low Pastures.

She went back into her bedroom. If there was going to be
a houseful of police, she'd better smarten up: important for

her image as well as Ralph's. Iles would notice any scruffiness, probably have a full-out giggle at it and expect his crawly troops to do the same.

She applied some swift improvements then went downstairs to stand with Ralph. Iles, in uniform, was still on the doorstep. Behind him she saw that other nuisance officer, Harpur, wearing plain clothes. And behind him the search people waited: a lot of search people.

'It's just routine, Margaret,' Ralph said, his voice steady.

'Certainly,' Iles said.

'Routine at four thirty in the morning?' she said.

'Routine in the sense that most of the search people here do many visits of this kind,' Iles said.

'How does that make it routine?' Margaret said.

'It's routine for *them*,' Iles said. 'These are what you might call 24/7 experts. They come into work of an evening and wonder to themselves, "What's on tonight?" And so they look at the briefing papers and murmur to one another, "A shake-down of Ralphy Ember's Low Pastures? Right." It's just another assignment to them. They don't feel any malice or antipathy. It could be anywhere, you see, Margaret.'

'But it isn't, is it?' Margaret said. 'It's here.'

'Ralph's name and address simply came up on the work-sheet,' Iles said.

'Who put it there? Why?' she said.

'It's done without vindictiveness, please believe me,' Iles replied.

'No,' Margaret said.

'No what?' Iles asked.

'No, I *don't* believe you,' she said.

'Work at it,' Iles said.

'What are you looking for?' Margaret said.

'Ah, what are we looking for? I hope we approach a search of this type with an open mind,' Iles said. 'It would surely pre-empt the very purpose of the search if we decided before the search took place what the search was trying to find. Our prime aim in an operation of this kind is fairness.'

'What *are* you trying to find?' Margaret said.

'This is why Harpur and I are here,' Iles replied.

'Why?' Margaret said.

'He won't answer queries, not sensibly,' Ember said.

'Are you set on fitting Ralph up for the Shale deaths?' Margaret said. 'Are you going to *find* something here, find something you brought? What is it? The gunman's business card – "Established 2010, Multiple Kills Catered For"? Who's got it to plant? Is there a trained expert at that kind of thing among your gang here?'

'He won't answer queries, not sensibly,' Ember said.

'Heterosexual women officers will, of course, do the girls' rooms,' Iles said. 'Officers familiar with, and uninflamed by, female garments.'

'How can you tell which rooms they are?' Margaret said.

'We felt it important when dealing with a property of this distinction to know our way around it before we arrived,' Iles said. 'That seemed only respectful and due.'

'I hear you're quite keen on young flesh yourself,' Margaret said.

'A remarkably fine residence, but not ideal as to security,' Iles replied. 'The fields, copses, hedges – a lot of approach cover. It would be quite a place to take care of – to defend – if Ralph were not around for a time.'

'But he *is* around,' she said.

'Well, yes,' Iles said.

'Suppose – suppose Ralph did have a lawless side. If he knew you were coming, you're not likely to find anything, are you, unless you've brought it yourselves?' Margaret said. 'He would have made sure the place is OK.'

'That's certainly a point,' Iles said.

Harpur said: 'How did you know about the call, Ralph?'

'Harpur sticks to a query,' Iles said. 'It's what got him to where he is. Many would admire the tenacity. I esteem him, even though, as you'll probably have heard, he deceitfully, lecherously—'

'You've got a stipended voice that talks to you from inside our building, have you, Ralph?' Harpur said.

SIX

The search split into three units: one downstairs, one up, one in the outbuildings. None found anything linked to the murders of Naomi Shale and the boy Laurent. Garland closed the operation at just before seven thirty a.m.

Standing in the doorway of Low Pastures, Margaret Ember yelled at the departing police vehicles: 'This was victimization. This was oppression. This was and is persecution!'

Iles nodded. At Margaret Ember's side, Ralph patted her gently on the shoulder, as if attempting to bring some calm. He looked vindicated, Hestonized, solid, grandly imperturbable. For the moment Harpur could not have connected him with that dismissive, earned nickname, Panicking Ralphy.

Margaret Ember had patrolled vigorously while the pry was under way, fixing herself for a while to each of the ferreting groups, then switching abruptly to another, then to the other, trying to catch one or more of them at some trickery. Garland had wanted her to be restricted to the Low Pastures hall, but the ACC overruled this. Although Iles might not be Gold tonight, he *was* Iles. Guidance came as diktat from him. 'It's her and Ralph's property, Francis. They must be able to move about in it, if they wish. They have affinities with and love these exposed beams, bare stone walls and showy, farcical fat-tomed library. Besides, I'm sure we've nothing to conceal, have we? An examination of our activities will prove them wholesome and well intentioned.'

Despite Margaret Ember's obvious hostility and rage, Harpur sensed she might wish to talk to him privately. Once, she had seemed about to approach, but Iles was near Harpur, exhaustively describing a Home Office administrator he considered shit; Iles considered most Home Office administrators shit, but this one exceptionally so, and therefore needing his character and appearance very thoroughly drawn. Margaret probably feared the ACC's involvement. Some people preferred

life without Iles's involvement. He would not have been able
to get his head around this, but it was true.

A while ago, Margaret Ember had come to see Harpur and
discuss her intention to walk out on Ralph with the children.
Harpur hadn't felt able to help her much, but he'd listened,
sympathized. Although she did her flit, she returned after only
several days. Was she thinking again about a dash, perhaps
staying away permanently this time? Would something like
the humiliating, irreverent, swarming, first-blush search of her
home shove her towards a new escape plan? Such resentment
might be coupled with alarm that Ralph, and therefore his
family, could be vengeance targets following the Shale deaths.
Did she need to talk about it again to somebody, somebody
like Harpur? She didn't come to speak with him, though, so
it was impossible to know as a certainty.

Iles and Harpur would go back to the debriefing at headquarters in an unmarked Peugeot from the pool. They walked
towards the car. Harpur said: 'This could be a very difficult
one for you, sir.'

'In which respect, Col?'

'Obviously, when the Chief hears Garland's report on the
circumstances – Ember fully dressed and ready for us, then a
wholly efficient, utterly useless, comb of the property . . . Yes,
when Sir Matthew hears this he's going to think you tipped
Ember off about the raid so he could get rid of anything
awkward.'

Iles sounded bored by the obviousness of this. 'Oh, that – of
course, of course. Poor, dear, thought-prone prick.'

'Would you say he was more prick than cunt, then, sir?'
Harpur said. 'This is an interesting distinction. You were always
very keen on precision.'

'He's someone who thinks he sees straight. They're always
sickeningly dangerous, Col.'

'There's the blessed, unspoken concordat between you,
Ralph and Shale, isn't there? Or there was, before Manse opted
out. You look after one another. This must colour Sir Matthew's
judgement on what's just happened and generally. Looking
after one another can have all sorts of meanings and
applications.'

'Certainly, Col,' Iles said. They boarded the Peugeot. They had no driver. Harpur was at the wheel. As they turned away from the front of Low Pastures on to the fine, curved driveway, Iles gave his thoughtful, nodded acknowledgement through the open passenger window to Margaret Ember's sun-up abuse screech.

'The Chief will see it as especially intelligent, and therefore wholly in line with what he expects from you, sir, that Ralph didn't put on a big yawn and nightshirt act, pretending he'd been roused from sleep,' Harpur said. 'Instead, he showed he'd known what would happen, and exactly when it would, by coming to the door dressed and announcing to you yourself he'd been forewarned.'

'Ralph has depths.'

'Sir Matthew might regard that as a fine double-bluff, mightn't he?'

'He's a prey to obsessions.'

'It takes care of the suspicion that Ember could have been alerted, but suggests someone else, not you, did the leaking. On the face of it, Ralph's hardly going to announce to the person who gave him the whisper that he'd been given a whisper, is he, sir?'

'Hardly, Col, on the face of it.'

'Unless he was coached by someone extraordinarily smart and subtle to announce to the very person who gave him the whisper that he'd been given a whisper. The double-bluff.'

'Yes, that's probably how Upton will see it, in his footling, top-rank, infantile, paranoid way.'

'You, sir, not technically in charge of the operation, yet taking over the doorbell-ringing, so you'd be the first person Ralph saw on the step.'

'It's the kind of magnificent, metal studded, *Wuthering Heights*-type of front door that needs a heavy iron knocker modelling a gorilla's head, not some piddling modern dulcet chime job,' Iles replied.

'And then the Chief is going to hear from Garland that Ralph continually asked what it was all about, as if entirely flummoxed. Sir Matthew will think that's done by Ember at your suggestion, sort of scenarioed and rehearsed for the occasion.'

'Inevitably.'

'Can you put up with this distrust from him, sir?'

'In a while, I think I might become quite fond of Sir Matt. He's someone who knows his own mind and yet is not ashamed of it. I admire that kind of courage.'

'I don't know where I stand on this,' Harpur replied.

'Which?'

'Whether you told Ralph on the quiet that we'd be coming and when, so as to mess up the Chief's strategy before it even got properly started. Pre-emptive.'

'It *is* a tricky one, isn't it, Col?'

'I can see likelihoods on both sides of the question.'

'You're not one to rush to judgement.'

'Thank you, sir.'

'If you eventually decide after this non-rush that I *didn't* have a pre-word with Ember, it would clearly be best to say nothing along those lines to the Chief, Col.'

'Which lines?'

'Defending me, testimonializing me, attempting to protect me at this jaw-jaw we're on our way to.'

'Surely it would be helpful if—'

'Don't champion me. Your support would only help convince Upton even more that he's interpreting things right.'

'I don't at all see—'

'He knows you would feel compelled to back me.'

'Not if I thought you probably *had* been in pre-touch with Ralph. That's serious treachery.'

Iles began to shout-scream and had trouble getting enough air into his lungs, although the passenger window remained down. They were in traffic, moving slowly. It was the morning rush-hour. People on the pavement, intrigued by the yelling, turned to stare at him and the Peugeot. They were used to fucking awful thump music booming through car windows, not a frenzied, inflamed live voice. 'Do I have to mention Sarah?' Iles said.

'Your wife, sir? Surely she doesn't have any part in—'

'My wife. Upton hears you repeatedly closed with my wife – that is, let's define what's what, shall we? – an *Assistant Chief's* wife. Yes, an Assistant Chief (Operation's) wife. You rakehelled with her in numerous undignified and often deeply déclassé settings. He'll assume, because he's a typical half-soaked gent with a Humanities degree, that you are now ashamed and wish to make paltry amends, compensate, by siding with me in any tough situation.'

Harpur said: 'Are you sure this is how the Chief would react? Isn't that a rather special way of reading things, sir?'

'It *is* a rather special way of reading things, Harpur, because it's *my* fucking way.'

'But there's a much wider policy matter here, sir, isn't there?' Harpur said.

'Certainly, Col.'

'You think conditions on our ground will be best if Ralph continues untroubled in business, alongside Manse's successor.'

'Certainly, Col.'

'The Chief wants Ralph wiped out, as first move in a general cleansing of our ground.'

'Sir Matthew is in many, many ways an almost acceptable figure but hasn't been in post long enough to appreciate the complexities of matters in this region, Col. I'll nurse him away from his predictable, corny new-brooming towards clarity. This is a chore, but it's the least I can do for the confused sod.'

'But your argument about tolerating the dealers is more general, more national – international, in fact – than just our region. You consider that if your methods worked here, they would be a model for countries everywhere. That's what I meant by "wider policy".'

'True. We have some very particular circumstances here, though,' Iles explained.

For instance, you, sir? But Harpur did not say this.

'In due course, Sir Matt will probably come to get the feel of how we run things. I do detect a quotient of brain power in him now and then, or even oftener. His degree is from somewhere making a real effort to get reputable, I hear. He's quite open about it.'

'You very generously said he wasn't a cunt, sir, though possibly a prick, and you're not somebody to scatter compliments carelessly.'

'If there's one quality I prize above most others it's balance,

Col. My mother would often remark on this quality in me, even when a child. "Desmond!" she'd exclaim, "you are *so* judicious."'

'I'd never say anything against someone's mother. People can be very touchy about their mothers.'

The Chief had already arrived when they reached headquarters. He was heavily built, plump rather than burly. He listened while Francis Garland reported, and then took versions of what had gone on from each of his team. Iles and Harpur listened, also. Garland gave a full narrative of events from arrival to departure, recounting conversations, explaining that Ember was in his day clothes, detailing his and Margaret's attitude. The search-trained officers said they'd been called by colleagues to anything that might seem significant in and around Low Pastures, but all were dead ends.

The Chief had made some notes. 'Have I got this right, Mr Garland? You arrived at the front door of Low Pastures at four thirty a.m.'

'Yes, sir,' Garland said.

'Ember had been given no official forewarning?' Upton said.

'Not to my knowledge,' Garland said. 'Forewarning would be completely inappropriate. Surprise was crucial.'

'And if there *had* been an official forewarning it would have come from you, or someone deputed by you, wouldn't it?' Upton said.

'I would have assumed so, yes, sir,' Garland said.

'I would have assumed so, also,' Upton said. 'Is that how you see things, too, Desmond?'

'No alternative,' Iles said unhesitatingly.

'I needed your view,' Upton said. He had a mild, insistent voice which Harpur had decided a while back linked to a very systematic mind. His hair was present in full, no thinning or grey in the fairish mass. His square, fleshy face matched his body structure. He had a broad, short nose, dark-blue eyes, heavy lips and a four-square chin. He was in shirt sleeves, his arms surprisingly slender. He had just reached forty-eight. 'So, you turned up, on the face of it quite unannounced as far as Ember and his family were concerned, and Mr Iles rang the front doorbell?' He sounded cheery and encouraging, as though leading someone into a description of an amusing incident in his or her life.

'That's so,' Garland said.

'Theoretically, Mr Iles was not part of the operation, I believe, and attended as a spectator only,' Upton said. 'He was, naturally, entitled to come along, as was Mr Harpur. But you had command. You were Gold for this operation?'

'I was Gold, yes, sir.'

'Oh, yes, no question, sir,' Iles said. 'Francis had charge. As I think I may have mentioned, his morals are not of the most charming – dick-driven – but he is a capable officer and in some aspects quite trustworthy, if you catch him on the right day.'

Upton consulted his notes. 'He led the operation, but you, Desmond, rang the doorbell, I gather.'

'I suppose one could say I did that as a kind of gesture,' Iles said. He was seated at a conference table but stood briefly now, leaned forward and with the index finger of his right acted out the decisive pressing of a bell. Then he took his chair again.

'What kind of gesture?' Upton said.

'Or perhaps term it an impulse,' Iles replied.

'How did you ring?' Upton said.

'There was a button marked "Press", black lettering on white. Several of our people had torch beams on the door. Locating the button and realizing its purpose were not difficult. You'll remember in *Alice* that she comes to a bottle marked "Drink Me", so she drinks it. It was the same for me with the button marked "Press". I pressed it.'

'No, when I ask how did you ring, I mean what, as it were, *shape* of ringing did you employ? What *pattern*? Was it simply one period of pressure on the button, as your miming just now seemed to indicate, or did you have a pattern of peals – say, for instance, two short rings or even three, or perhaps one long and two shorts, or six or seven short jabs like in the childish chant: "Dat-di-da-da-da-da. Hi-diddledy batch cakes, brown bread."'

Iles said: 'I remember it rather as the first line of the song: "How's your father? All right: slept in the dustbin all night."'

Such cheerful, inconsequential days, boyhood. Do you feel nostalgic about those times, sir? I certainly do.'

'And Ralph Ember, fully dressed, more or less instantly responded to the bell?' Upton replied.

'He did,' Garland said.

'It can be stated, then, that your *gesture* worked very well, Desmond,' Upton said.

'I think I can claim to have rung with due force,' Iles said, 'though I'm not here to claim that if someone else had pressed the bell, matters would have been different. Just the one, long, plain-speaking ding, however – without subsequent fiddly additions. No need for any special, pre-agreed warning signal, was there, sir?'

'No, indeed,' Upton said.

'What would I wish to warn him of?' Iles replied.

'Quite,' Upton said. 'Oh, quite. Now, I can, of course, see that Ember's prompt appearance in day attire might not be totally exceptional, because he is a club owner and no doubt is kept late on some special nights there.'

'He does have occasional trouble persuading people to quit The Monty, despite the sty that it is,' Iles said. 'I rather like the French word for doorman or bouncer – it's *videur*, as you probably know, sir. A chucker-out. An emptier! Often, Ralph could do with a couple of those.'

Upton said: 'And then we have your introductory words to him, Desmond, as reported by Francis Garland just now. I wrote these as: "Ralph, here's a treat!"'

'It might well have been a cry of that sort,' Iles said. 'Something matey and exuberant to take away a little of the shock and unpleasantness of our arrival pre-breakfast.'

'And yet it does not appear to have been a shock at all, does it?' Upton said. 'In a sense, anti-shock, flagrantly non-shock, since he was totally prepared.'

'One couldn't have forecast that,' Iles said.

'Possibly not,' Upton said. 'Possibly not. First-name terms?'

'It's how it is with people like Ember,' Iles said.

'"People like Ember" being?' Upton said.

'That's quite a tricky one, sir. Ember is very various,' Iles said. 'I think most here would agree with this.'

'People like Ember are rare, thank God,' Upton said. His voice became steely and purposeful. 'They are shameless, large-scale, ruthless, moneyed traders in illegal substances, and most likely parties to all types of criminal violence connected with their business, including the murder of a woman and child. They mix what they call "bash" with the cocaine they trade – traditionally uncostly stuff like baby milk powder or caffeine, but now potentially dangerous pharmaceutical products such as benzocaine – to fool customers and hugely increase profits.'

'We're working on the murders, sir,' Iles said.

'But it's Ember's answer to your greeting that surely is bound to stand out, Desmond,' Upton said. '"I'd heard you'd be calling at around this time today." I have this right, too?'

'That's how he responded, yes, sir,' Iles said.

'Yes,' Garland said.

'"I'd heard," he says. But how could he have heard?' Upton asked. 'Not simply that there would be a raid, but the time and date. Had there been gossip outside the team?'

'I'd ordered complete silence. My people would understand that need,' Garland said. 'We do this sort of unheralded visit as virtually standard. And the confidentiality is standard, also.'

'The blatant and complete failure of that confidentiality here must make for some uneasiness, mustn't it?' the Chief said.

'Unquestionably,' Iles replied at once.

'And Mr Harpur expressed uneasiness at once, didn't he?' Upton said.

'That kind of directness, meat-and-potatoes frankness, is typical of Col,' Iles replied. 'It's not necessarily naive.'

'I make it that he raised the matter three times,' Upton said, looking again at his notes.

'He'd persist. That also is typical,' Iles said.

'With finally the statement,' Upton said, and read out: '"You've got a stipended voice that talks to you from inside our building, have you, Ralph?"'

'Stipended, yes,' Iles said. 'Harpur can come up with some quaint vocab. He's more or less self-educated, and when the self is his kind of self there are going to be some odd results, aren't there, sir?'

'What exactly did you mean, Mr Harpur?' Upton replied.

'I'd assume he was suggesting some officer had been long-term bought by Ralph Ember and supplied him regularly with confidential material,' Iles said.

'What exactly did you mean, Mr Harpur?' Upton replied.

'Yes, as the Assistant Chief suggests,' Harpur said.

'Someone bought?' Upton said.

'Yes,' Harpur said.

'This would be a grave offence, wouldn't it? Perverting the course of justice,' Upton said.

'Yes,' Harpur said.

'Certainly,' Iles said.

'You think money would be involved – bribery?' Upton said.

'Almost definitely,' Harpur said.

'Almost? There could be some other reason, in your view?' Upton said.

'It's possible,' Harpur said.

'How would you intend to deal with the matter?' Upton said.

'There must be inquiries,' Harpur said.

'You have to identify this source,' Upton said.

'Yes,' Harpur said.

'This source had impeccable knowledge of our raid plans,' Upton said.

'Clearly,' Harpur said.

'Certainly,' Iles said.

'That should limit the possibles,' Upton said. 'Someone exceptionally well placed.'

'Yes,' Harpur said.

'It's a situation putting a shadow on everyone who had pre-info on the raid, isn't it, Mr Harpur?' Upton said.

'It is,' Harpur said.

'How do *you* feel about it, Mr Garland?' Upton said.

'It *is* uncomfortable,' Garland said.

'Desmond?' Upton replied.

'Affronted,' Iles said. 'Utterly. It is contemptible behaviour.'

'You spoke of trying to lessen the shock for Ember in this

early morning visit, but were you, yourself, shocked by his statement that he'd been expecting you?' Upton said.

'Massively,' Iles said.

'A very natural reaction, if I may say. Did you question him about it, in the way Mr Harpur did?' Upton asked.

'People like Ember are unlikely to answer such a question – answer it truthfully,' Iles said.

'Ah, we have that phrase again,' Upton replied.

'Which phrase, sir?' Iles said.

'"People like Ember",' the Chief said. 'What are people like Ember like, in your opinion, Desmond?'

Iles chuckled and gave the table a small blow with his fist. 'It's remarkable you should ask this, sir, because, as a matter of fact, Ember has a plaque on one of the gates at Low Pastures hinting at that very need, the need to define personality,' he said. 'Of course, you'll recall it from your undergrad days at . . . yes, your undergrad days: *Mens cuiusque is est quisque.*' Cicero being Mr Fucking Cleverclogs with all those Qs, but not clever enough. He tells us a man's mind is what the man is, but he doesn't tell us how to find out what a man's mind might be up to.'

'You think Mr Harpur was wasting his efforts asking Ember how he knew everything about the operation?' Upton replied.

'Col has his style of dealing with things,' Iles said. 'It's more or less unarguable that he has had successes. And I stress the plural.'

SEVEN

There would be two more killings. Possibly, they proved Upton's analysis of things right and Iles's wrong. Or the opposite. Upton might say that wherever large-scale drug dealing went on – tolerated or not – violence was sure to accompany it, and so Iles's attempt to achieve civic peace through a bargain with the main outfits would ultimately fail. Against this, Iles might say that once the law started monkeying with the type of arrangement he favoured, or even talking about those kinds of changes, firms would get scared and lash out, trying to protect themselves. Harpur couldn't settle in his head which of them had things correct.

And – another sweet uncertainty – could he have prevented the two deaths? He'd had the warning, hadn't he? There'd been that surprising conversation backed by tea and currant loaf while the kids were at judo. Should he have done something, something life-preserving? At the time, it had seemed impossible. He didn't feel so sure when confronted by those deaths and looking back. Perhaps he'd treated the tip-off casually because of where it came from, and how it came. Had he begun to get slack?

On the day of this conversation he'd been just about to get into the car with his daughters. The two deaths were still a long way ahead then, of course. Jill said quietly: 'Over there, Dad, someone hanging around in the street. I've seen her from the window, as well. Twenty-fiveish. Fair-to-mousy cowlick. No lipstick. Denim top and jeans. Purple slingbacks. I think she wants to talk to you.' Jill didn't point but gave a small, almost unnoticeable nod towards her. 'You know this person at all?'

Harpur looked. 'No.' But, yes, though only from dossier pictures and profiling: Karen Lister, live-in girlfriend of one of Mansel Shale's top people, Jason Ivan Claud Wensley. Harpur's daughters always worried that some woman he'd never told

them about would turn up and make Denise hurt enough, and
jealous enough, and angry enough to ditch him. If she ditched
him, she'd ditch them, too. They obviously considered him
lucky to have kept her this long. He wouldn't argue. They wanted
him to be careful. They wanted him to behave right. They tried
to watch him as much as they could, which they knew wasn't
very much at all. They wondered what went on when they
couldn't, which they knew was often. They'd been forced to
learn about family frailty. It made them suspicious and jumpy.

Harpur was just going to drive them to the judo club. Hazel
said: 'Yes, I've noticed her, too, Dad. She looks really anxious.
She brings trouble for someone, I think.'

'For Dad?' Jill said.

'For someone,' Hazel said.

'Very slim,' Jill said. Harpur interpreted: not at this point
accusingly belly-bulged, up-the-duff. 'Very slim, but also
boobs,' Jill said.

'She could be looking for almost anyone,' Harpur said. 'So
many of the houses in this street are multi-flatted and poorly
occupant-labelled.' Sometimes he'd try to crush his daughters
with a gross pile of ugly, lifeless syllables.

'Yes, she *could* be looking for almost anyone, but she isn't,
unless you're almost anyone,' Hazel said. 'Which I suppose
you could be mistaken for, though.'

Karen Lister was a little way down the street on the other
side. When the three came out of the house, she had been
right opposite, but began to walk away fast. 'There,' Harpur
said. 'She's not concerned with us.'

'Of course she's concerned with us,' Hazel said. 'We appear
on the doorstep and she belts off, pretending *not* to be
concerned with us because she is.'

'Look,' Jill said.

Lister had stopped, as if suddenly hit by a change of mind;
maybe by shame at having chickened. She turned, crossed the
street and approached them quickly. 'This is luck,' she said,
with a very nice, hearty boom to her voice.

'What is?' Harpur said.

'Luck?' Hazel said. 'Excuse me, but only an idiot could
call this luck, or someone putting on an act.'

'I'm delighted to have bumped into you, Mr Harpur,' the woman said. 'It *is* Mr Harpur, isn't it?'

'You know it is,' Hazel said.

'Bumped into him?' Jill said. 'Is this "bumped into him"?'

'Mr Harpur, could we talk somewhere for a couple of minutes?' Karen Lister replied. She meant privately, without the children. Her tone said it. The boom and phoney heartiness were for him only. 'I recognized you from TV news.'

'Well,' Harpur said, 'I'm afraid I have to take—'

'Is this something urgent?' Jill asked her. 'Yes, it must be, mustn't it, or why lurk here?'

'I'm Karen Lister,' she replied.

'Should Dad know this name?' Jill said.

'Karen Louise Lister.'

'Dad knows all sorts,' Jill said.

'You might recognize the name, Mr Harpur,' Karen Lister said.

'Dad? Do you? He can go very shutters-up sometimes,' Jill said. 'That's partly from the job, but in any case he's like that. Into secrets. He does blankness. Have you noticed that in him, I wonder?'

'We're due elsewhere,' Harpur said. 'Could you call at my office tomorrow if it's a work matter?'

'I don't go to police stations,' she said.

'Ever?' Jill said. 'What if your bike's pinched, or the Labrador lost?'

'Would I want to be seen going to a police station?' Karen Lister enjoyed a small laugh, as though going to a police station would be as mad as high-diving into a fruit bowl or joining the Labour Party.

'Would you?' Hazel said. 'Why not? That's what police stations are for – so people can go to them.'

'I think I understand what she means, Haze,' Jill said.

'Oh, *you* would,' Hazel said.

'It's not so very unusual, believe me,' Jill replied.

'Tell us about it, do,' Hazel said.

'She has a special way of thinking about police stations,' Jill said. 'It's special, but it's also quite common.'

'What special way?' Hazel replied.

'This is like in *omertà*,' Jill said. 'But, Karen – OK to call you Karen? – Karen, you're afraid someone might find out you've been spilling to police, are you?'

'Oh, *omertà*!' Hazel said. 'This is crazy. She's the Mafia, the Godmother?'

'You know some dangerous folk, do you, Karen?' Jill said. 'Dad's used to that kind of thing. And then there's someone called Iles who's quite good at those carry-ons, too – squashing villains. Maybe you've heard of him. He could be a reason you don't like going into police stations, because he might be there, being an Assistant Chief. Although not everybody believes it, really deep in his being Des Iles has got what's known as integrity, meaning OKness, and, like a gent, he's given up chasing Haze, who's still not sixteen, because he found she had a serious boyfriend her own age, Des Iles being married with a child.'

'Mouth,' Hazel replied.

'I took the risk of coming to your district, Mr Harpur,' Karen Lister said. 'I watched the rear mirror.'

'It's just as obvious as visiting the nick,' Hazel said, 'pacing about like that, pretending you've got somewhere to go when it's obvious you haven't.'

'I'll drop the girls off at judo and return straight away,' Harpur said. 'Can you come to the house in half an hour?'

'She's afraid of being noticed by those dangerous people I mentioned, Dad,' Jill said. 'She should come with us in the car, and then you can drive her back, or talk in the car. That might be best – talk in the car.'

The girls would think there'd be time to give Karen Lister a proper, intensive vetting if she joined them now on the ride to judo. And they'd try to make sure that, never mind what they discovered about her then, she didn't go back to Arthur Street with him. Karen Lister had a good body, slim only where it ought to be slim. His daughters might not like the notion of Harpur and her in the house on their own. Denise wouldn't be there until later. She'd said she had crawl coaching at the university pool this evening.

'Yes, all right, I'll come back to the house,' Karen Lister said. Harpur had the idea she didn't want to be celled in the car with these kids and their wonderings and probes.

Jill said: 'But you might get spotted waiting in Arthur Street. Hazel and I picked you out. It's to do with what's known as "body language". I don't know if you've ever come across that phrase.'

'I left my Mini around the corner. I'll wait in that,' Karen Lister replied.

'That's fine then,' Harpur said. 'See you at 126 shortly.'

Karen Lister moved away from the car and resumed her walk.

On the drive to judo, Hazel said: 'She seems really very interesting in some ways.'

'Well, yes,' Harpur said.

'I don't see how she can be interesting if we don't know anything about her, except she's not fond of nicks,' Jill said. 'There's plenty like that, and not just on account of *omertà*.'

'It's *because* we don't know anything much about her that she's interesting,' Hazel said. 'Why was she keeping stuff from us?'

'Which stuff?' Jill said.

'That's what I'm getting at, Thicko,' Hazel said. 'There's stuff she's not telling us, and this makes us wonder what this stuff is. So, we're interested. If you think about, say, a vicar with a sermon, we're not interested because we've heard it all before and he puts it out again in front of us. But with this Karen Lister, she's holding something back, and we'd like to get at it and to know why she's holding it back.'

'Although you didn't recognize her at first, Dad, I was wondering if as soon as she talked to us you suddenly remembered who she was,' Jill said. 'It's well known that can happen with people's memories – they may be given a jab by something, and it all comes back to them. Say, for instance, when she spoke her name.'

'If it's her true name,' Hazel replied.

'The memory can do some weird things, yes,' Harpur said.

'Or it might be perfume,' Jill said.

'What might be?' Hazel said.

'It's also well known that we could be looking at something and not able to remember it, such as a face and so on, or listening to a voice and not remembering that either, but then another sense takes over from sight and hearing, that is, the nose, and smelling something particular with it, a familiar scent, or once familiar,' Jill said. 'And this causes the memory to wake up and bring everything back, not just the memory of the smell, but the whole thing. This smell sort of opens a door to all sorts of other things in the memory, like opening the door to a pantry. I don't think the scent she had on today was too bad. It might have been her favourite for a long while – such as Chanel's "Allure", or "Red" by Giorgio Beverly Hills – and when somebody gets a whiff of it now it is as though time returns, like, automatically to the first day or night he or she met the smell of this scent, sketching out that whole earlier scene, which is very helpful in the matter of recalling. Yes, Dad, memory is rather a tricky item.'

'You don't need "like, automatically",' Harpur replied. '"Automatically" will do.'

'Did that scent send your mind back automatically to the first time you smelled it one day?' Jill said. 'Or, of course, night. Some women do more scent at night owing to social-izing and so on. I think she'd be an Allure fan.'

'No,' Harpur said.

'No, what?' Jill said. 'You think, not Allure? Something else? Red? Or something else altogether? You know, do you? Which scent was it, then?'

'No, I didn't recognize her scent – any scent,' Harpur said. 'How could I if I've never met her?' And scent wouldn't figure in her file.

'That's what we're talking about, isn't it, Dad?' Jill replied.

'What?'

'*Did* you know her, but have forgotten you knew her, and the scent might remind you you knew her,' Jill said, 'leading to a complete memory of that previous meeting? This is the kind of thing memory can do. Why I said "tricky".'

'No,' Harpur said.

'Why didn't she just ring up and arrange to see you, Dad, not street-loiter?' Hazel said. 'We're in the book.'

'Some people don't trust phones,' Jill said.

'So she displays herself in Arthur Street instead? If she was wearing sandwich boards with "I'm looking for Col Harpur" on she wouldn't have been more obvious,' Hazel said. 'She leaves her car out of sight, so you might think she knew something about security and undercover, but then she struts along in front of the house, and then struts away from the house so fast anyone would know she's only in the street because of number 126.'

'Desperate people do things that aren't always very brainy,' Jill replied. 'She said she "bumped into" Dad, though we know she'd been on the prowl, so that wasn't very brainy either. I suppose she had to say *something* to explain why she was there. But because of stress she chose something stupid.'

'Do you think she's to do with the Shale situation, Dad?' Hazel said.

'This is a case with many sides,' Jill replied.

'There *are* difficulties with it,' Harpur said.

'If you regard her as just a nuisance, there's no need to go back to the house immediately, even though it's arranged,' Jill said. 'She'll call there, but if you didn't show she'd realize that wasn't the way you wanted to do things, such as a police matter, a work matter. It should be dealt with at the nick. Too bad she doesn't like going there. If she wants something she got to follow the right procedure. Pity she's not here now. I'd say, "Sorry, Karen, but that's the picture."'

'*Has* to follow the right procedure,' Harpur replied.

'Yes, she has to,' Jill said.'

'I believe she's a moll of some sort,' Hazel said.

'What's that?' Jill said.

'In a crook's crew, or partner of a crook,' Hazel said. 'It's the mixture of breeziness and nerves. These I noted in her.'

'I'll probably see her briefly at home,' Harpur replied.

'I don't think it's wise, Dad,' Jill said.

'Why?' he said.

'It doesn't seem . . . well, it doesn't seem very suitable, that's all,' Jill said.

'Why?' Harpur said.

'Yes, unsuitable,' Jill said.

'I agree with Hazel,' Harpur replied. 'This woman has troubles. We're here to give help when there are troubles.'

'Which "we" is that?' Jill said.

'Police,' Harpur said.

'Or what if Ilesy suddenly calls at 126, like, not expected one bit, the way he does?' Jill said. 'Even now when he's not after Haze any longer and flashing his crimson scarf.'

'Creature,' Hazel replied.

'So?' Harpur said.

'You're there with another woman in the house, not old. Older than Denise, but not old,' Jill said. 'Purple slingbacks. Boobs.'

'In the way of business,' Harpur said.

'He'll believe that?' Jill said. 'This is why I say unsuitable.'

Harpur pulled in at the judo. 'Pick you up here at the usual time,' he said.

'Maybe I should come back with you now,' Jill said. 'Haze can stay. If Des Iles called in it would be all right then, because I'd be in the house as well, saying I had to miss judo because too much homework.'

'No, it will be fine,' Harpur said. He put their sports bags out on the pavement.

'You seem in quite a hurry,' Jill said.

Of course it pissed him off now and then, this obsession of theirs with women he met, but he understood where their uneasiness came from and so didn't show he resented it and felt monitored by it. If you were the single parent in a single parent family, you ought to try to avoid too much single-parent rattiness, otherwise the children would come to regard rattiness as natural to being a parent: they'd have no other current experience of parenthood for comparison. He drove back to the house and tidied up the place a bit.

Although, these days, he liked the big sitting-room, it used to darken his soul and cause him shortness of breath when Megan was alive because she had her books on hardwood shelves, floor to ceiling, around all four walls. He thought the spine-names on some of these pitiless volumes would have depressed almost anyone, not just himself. He kept a few of the titles fully and accurately in his head so he could relish the fact they'd been carted away free on a strictly non-return basis by a dealer. It used to buck him up when he felt forlorn

if he made his mind recall, one by fucking one, these gloriously gone works: *Old Fortunatus*, *The Rules and Exercises
of Holy Dying*, *Edwin Drood*, *The Virtues of Sid Hamet the
Magician's Rod*, *U And I*. He'd had the shelves removed, and
the room redecorated, a decent, respectful while after Megan's
death. It would have been crude and unfeeling to do an immediate chuck.

Jill had wanted a couple of the collection for herself – one
on boxing, *The Sweet Science*, and one the diary of a play-
wright called Orton – but the rest went. He would have hated
for this woman, Karen Lister, to come into the house seeking
help and get unnerved, even panicked, by sight of that smug,
engulfing, interminable book depot.

He drew the curtains after he led Karen in. She'd expect
that. The sitting room had windows on to the street, and she
wanted this visit discreet, not blatant under lights. It was usual
to close the curtains on autumn and winter evenings, so the
kids would not be able to kick up about crafty concealment
for something sexual.

Karen Lister said: 'I'm trying to work out where you stand
in all this.'

'All which?'

'The drugs tableau.'

'I'm a police officer.'

'So is the one called Iles mentioned by your daughter.
Everyone knows he has his own views re drugs. He thinks
decriminalize, doesn't he, with more money for treatment?
Like in Portugal.'

'Mr Iles is concerned with big-time strategy.'

'How about you?'

'I'm a police officer.'

'And then this new Chief,' she replied. 'A dawn raid on
Ralphy Ember's house. You were there, weren't you, and Iles,
although the operation was run by someone else. Symbolic,
your and Iles's presence? So, where are we?'

'Gossip gets around.'

'When I say, "Where are we?" what I mean is, are Ralphy
Ember and his firm to be wiped out?'

Yes, if Upton could manage it, Ember was to be eliminated

as first stage in something larger. 'I'd be interested to know where you pick up your rumours,' he said.

'The changes – potential changes – bewilder me,' she said. 'They're frightening.'

He made tea and served it in proper china cups decorated with blue leaves and tendrils, plus matching saucers. He was keen on china and thought he might do some systematic study and buying when he retired. He loved how, with the best examples, something solid like the side of a cup could be almost transparent.

'So?' Hazel had said when he spoke admiringly of it one day. His daughters considered this interest an affectation and 'salon snobby', as Hazel termed it. Jill didn't seem to get what 'salon' meant, but she agreed about the snobbery. He'd seen them pour tea out of the cups he'd used when they had company and into stubby beige mugs.

For the meeting with Karen Lister, he'd also marged some slices of currant bread and arranged these on a large plate from the same set. She seemed to enjoy the snack. Hazel usually made sure some of the bread in the cupboard was reasonably fresh.

'You've got a file on me, I expect,' Karen Lister said.

'I deliberately don't go ex-directory so that anyone with a problem who thinks I might be useful can look me up in the book and get in touch,' Harpur replied. 'I'm glad you took advantage of that.'

'I try to imagine what that file would record,' she said. '*Karen Louise Lister, born January 1985, no convictions, live-in girlfriend-slash-partner of Jason Ivan Claud Wensley, number three or possibly four in the Shale hierarchy.* There might be amendments to that last part since Manse has withdrawn. Jason's probably number two now, after Michael Redvers Arlington, aka General Franco.'

Yes, as far as Harpur could recall, the entry might be something like that. It would be brief, with little on her physical appearance. She signified only as a side item to the boyfriend: no need for a lot of identification stuff. Jill was right about the fair-to-mousy cowlick. Behind it, the rest of her hair hung straight to just above her shoulders. Jill was also right about the slimness, along, though, with what she called 'boobs'. Lister had dark-blue eyes, a short-nosed, wary looking, strong cheek-boned face, fine skin, full lips, and small, even teeth. It all assembled into something as near to beautiful as anyone was likely to get. But he doubted whether that wary look was wary *enough*. Did she know how she was risking herself? That is, *really* know. She knew it sort of logically, theoretically, and had kept alert in case she had a tail. But did she know the perils in the way real perils were known – by feeling them continuously at her centre, a non-stop burn?

With corpses, he'd always found a display of small, regular teeth in a part-open mouth especially awful, as though that mouth still wanted to say something, perhaps joke, or amend, or bite a slice of currant loaf.

She sat straight-backed on the chesterfield, occasionally lifting or replacing her cup and saucer on a coffee table. She'd be about five foot nine inches tall, getting towards six feet in the slingbacks. Her accent wasn't local. He thought maybe anglicized, educated Welsh.

'That assault on Low Pastures – people are bound to ask what it signifies, aren't they,' she said, 'after all the previous non-intervention by Iles and the rest of you. It's like ravaging a cathedral. Until now, a kind of reverence for the place, Ralphy and Margaret Ember's shrine. Iles looks after them, just as he tried to look after Manse Shale. All right, the Embers can be charming, perhaps earn some special treatment. There's Ralph with the young Chuck Heston glow. And Margaret is sweet – gave us a lift home one night from The Monty when we'd drunk too much celebrating someone's suspended sentence.'

'*Which* people are bound to ask?'

'Two possibilities lie behind all this, don't they? Maybe three?' she said. 'First, Ralphy has upset Iles somehow, so that's the end of tolerance. This would devastate Margaret. Second, Iles has been overruled by your new Chief who hates the ACC's blind-eye drugs policy and will work to end it, and make you and he work to end it: maybe the new Chief has been posted here with particular orders to smash the drugs set-up. Third, Iles has himself lost belief in that policy – maybe

because of the Shale killings – and decided permissiveness
doesn't function after all.'

'You study these things, do you?' Harpur said.

'I study them because some of us might get hurt.'

'Which "us" is that?'

'Us. Me, for instance. My partner, Jason Wensley. You'll
have a bigger file on him.'

Yes, there was a hefty dossier on Jason, and, besides this,
Harpur had seen him now and then around Valencia Esplanade
and other drug-dealing spots in what seemed some sort of
managerial, whipper-in role. 'Ah, files,' he said. 'Police are
turning into bureaucrats. RIP Dirty Harry.'

'I'd love to see what you've got re Jason.'

'Does he know you've come here to talk to me?' Harpur
replied.

She stared at him across the considerable segment of currant
loaf on its way to her teeth, which she halted now. 'Of course
he doesn't,' she said. 'What would I tell him? How would I
put it? "Oh, by the way, Jase, I'm popping over to see that
charming cop, Harpur, and will let him know I'm scared more
or less paralytic in case you get killed because of your plotting, and would like him to intervene and prevent it."' She
completed the bread move and munched slowly, as though she
thought she had squashed Harpur by this surge of sarcasm and
could now concentrate on her vittles.

'You're acting solely as you?' he asked.

'I'm acting solely as me, but because I fret about *him*. He's
got some scheme. He's got some associates. They hobnob on
the quiet. They're preparing something.'

'The plotting?' Harpur found his own frets growing, but for
her. He felt pretty certain he would have been as concerned
even if she'd been plain, with poor legs. Or he hoped that was
true. Anything other would be debased. She sat very upright.
Her legs, slantwise and together, but not discouragingly
together, seemed to him how a woman's legs ought to be.
He'd prefer that Hazel and Jill didn't see her sitting like this.
'Will Jason wonder where you are?' he said. 'Will others
wonder where you are? The general scene is quite tense since
Sandicott and then Mansel's move out.'

'I could be anywhere. Around the shops? I'm not kept on a leash.'

'But you're not anywhere. You're here.'

'You think your house is watched?'

'I think *you* might be, Karen.'

'I said I paid attention to the mirror.'

'This is not the driving test. You could be dealing with very smart people who know every tailing trick. They don't cling close to your backside. They don't pose in your mirror. Then, there's your car, parked and standing a long while.'

'Among other cars. Not yelling for notice.'

'People in the noticing trade don't expect what they're looking for to yell at them. They notice what many would regard as unnoticeable.'

'I deliberately left it a distance from your house.'

'They might allow for that.'

'Oh, God, Harpur, you bring endless objections. Why would they imagine I might be flaky?'

'Some of them suspect everyone always. You might have given off signs you're not aware of.'

'You're saying I shouldn't have come?'

'Well, I'm—'

'I couldn't see what else to do.' She spoke it plain: no tremble or tears or face slump. She chewed more currant loaf. He felt pretty sure currant loaf didn't possess aphrodisiac qualities. 'You just told me you were here for people with difficulties,' she said. 'I have difficulties.'

That stabbed him. 'Stay put. I'll go and have a look at the street.' He left the house and walked a slow couple of hundred metres leftwards, but having a good all-directions gaze. He didn't see anything to perturb him. What the fuck did that mean, though? There were people about. A few he recognized as neighbours. The others meant nothing to him. Essentially, this stroll added up to that same nothing. Useless. Token. It was on a par with his later visits, revisits, to Sandicott Terrace. Gesture. Twitch. Pantomime. Let's-play-detective.

He tried to work out whether one or more of these unknowns seemed especially focused on him, or on the house. But members of that noticing trade he'd spoken of would take care they noticed without being noticed noticing: a basic skill. He might even be making things worse. He didn't often, if ever, do patrols on foot in Arthur Street and stare through 360 degrees. Would his absurd saunter flag up something exceptional? Did he look as though he might be on reconnaissance? If so, why was it needed? He mustn't prolong the stroll, anyway. He'd have to go and fetch his daughters soon.

'I mentioned a scheme. You'll ask what kind of scheme,' Karen Lister said when he returned. 'My partner Jason's scheme.'

'What kind of scheme?' Harpur said.

'If Ralph Ember's company is blitzed, no matter what the reason, there'll be increased possibilities for any firm that's not Ralph Ember's. This is Jason's thinking. Take Ember out and what's left – a vacuum where his outfit used to be?'

'Nature abhors a vacuum,' Harpur replied.

'These ancient maxims can tell us something occasionally. That's how Jason sees it, too,' she said. 'He wants to move in there, grab the abandoned territory, incorporate the excellent business structure built by Ralphy, establish monopoly. I think Jase has at least a couple of collaborators in on the project. But Jason's definitely kingpin. He originated the idea.'

So, Iles thought a vacuum because Shale had gone, and Karen's boyfriend, Wensley, thought a vacuum because Ember would go. Hell, Manse's withdrawal had brought big destabilization. Harpur found it tough to adjust.

'Look, I'm terrified,' she said. Again, no facial or body signs to signal inner anxiety.

Harpur said: 'So far nothing has—'

'I want you to talk to him, Mr Harpur – to Jason. You'll have our address in the files. I want you to show you're aware of his plans. That will stop him. I'm certain that will stop him, and his pals. He thinks the essence of any coup by him is surprise. The situation invites him in, and he must move immediately. He doesn't know much re such things – how could he? He's never been in this position before – but he's read a bit here and there. How all coups operate – surprise.'

'He discusses coups with you?'

'He talks a little. I know his mind. I can read him all right,

I think. I hope. My theory is, if he discovers you're in on it, he'll realize surprise is not available any longer, and he'll not go on. OK, you'll say now you're not, in fact, aware of his plans, or only this very vaguest outline I've just given you.'

Harpur said: 'I'm not, in fact, aware of his plans, or only this very vaguest outline you've just given me.'

'It shapes like this – and it's what shatters my nerves. Jason is where in the ex-Shale, new-Shale, organization? Number Two? Three? Either way, he's not the designated leader, that heir nominated by Manse. *He's* Michael Arlington, isn't he? All right, Arlington must have some strengths or Manse Shale wouldn't have picked him. But there are these wobbles of his mind, the General Franco, *El Caudillo*, complex. OK, spasms only, but potentially dangerous spasms. And who knows what they might develop into? He's got a Falangist civil guard's three-cornered hat, you know. Well, yes, of course you know. And you'll probably sense what comes next: Jason doesn't believe Arlington has the sustained judgement, strength and determination to manage the kind of operation needed. He's going to try to push him out. In a way, the logic is irresistible.'

'Which way?'

'Irresistible but perilous.'

'Push him out how?' Harpur replied.

'Yes, push him out.'

'Demote him?'

'More than that, I imagine. Jason would be afraid Arlington might make bother for him from the back-benches. It could be Arlington's turn to try a coup. It's what Franco did against the Popular Front government, isn't it?'

'You're saying Jason and his mates would kill Arlington?'

'And afterwards, Jason will run the show, maybe backed by his allies. He's got those three possibilities I listed to think about: maybe Iles has fallen out with Ralph and is going to get rid of him; maybe your new Chief has taken decision-making away from Iles; maybe Iles himself has concluded, post Sandicott, that the drugs scene has to be totally cleaned up. Whichever, Jason believes he can handle it and that General Franco couldn't.'

'And you?'

'What do I think? It's miles too dangerous. OK, Arlington has lapses, but he's bound to know how to protect himself. A bodyguard is almost always with him – Edison Something.'

'Whitehead,' Harpur said.

'Capable?'

'Experienced.'

'Loyal to Arlington?'

'As far as I know.'

'Arlington will be able to deal with any attempt at a putsch. As I've said, what familiarity with coups, with putsches, does Jase have? Why imagine he'd be any better at an internal struggle than Arlington? Think Madrid. Did any putsch against General Franco succeed once he got power? And in Spain, Franco didn't have Manse Shale backing him.'

'If I talk to Jason—'

'Tell him what you've heard and that it's stupid. If this new Chief is set on destroying not just Ralph's firm but what remains of Shale's as well, there'll be nothing for Jason or General Franco to lead. He – whichever – will be annihilated by the police under your new disinfecting boss. My own bet is that's what's happening, in fact. The Low Pastures raid was only a beginning. True? This Upton wants a totally pure domain. It's not a matter of Iles's turning against Ralph, nor of Iles changing attitude. This is a new Chief acting like a new Chief. He comes trailing clouds of clean-up.'

'That's poetic.'

'Nearly. Or he's been instructed to start a clean-up.'

She had an intellect, Karen Louise Lister, despite the 're's. She saw damn clearly. She'd be able to run a firm herself. Harpur said: 'If I talk to him, he'll obviously know I've been leaked to by someone.'

'By someone, yes.'

'Don't you think he'll know who?'

'You needn't say.'

'The only other possible would be one of his co-plotters. Why would they do that – give away a plan that could bring them fat money and power? No. You'll be top of the likelies.'

'Perhaps.'

'How would he react if he came to suspect you? What you're doing is a kind of betrayal, isn't it? This is his prized project and you aim to sabotage it.'

'He'd see I was trying to help him.'

'Don't count on that.'

'I'd like him to stay alive,' she replied.

In fact, Harpur thought she was taking risks for Wensley in a way he would almost certainly detest. That's how women could be. Governed by love – admirable; but their responses narrowed, simplified by love – sometimes, not so admirable. 'You also should try to stay alive,' Harpur told her. He felt reasonably certain he would have said that to anyone in Karen Lister's situation: it wasn't to do with her fine face and body. He still reckoned he'd achieved very considerable neutrality as regards those, and spoke to her as most police officers, of either sex, would speak to anyone who needed a warning about a hazard, hazards. In any case, she was fucking obviously and intensely committed to Jase. 'I have to go for the children now. I'll drive you to your car,' he said.

Did she seem hurt, let down, by this dismissal? 'Is that wise?' she said.

'I don't know a wise way for you to get to it, but it's got to be got to so you can go home as normal. Do a bit of token shopping en route?' He left the cups and saucers out and the remains of the bread. He felt there was something innocent looking about a currant loaf which might reassure Hazel and Jill. If an interlude had been innocent, proclaim this innocence. Make the most of it. Things would not always be so easy. A currant loaf was kiddies' picnic grub. It smelled of fruit, not sex. Definitely no aphrodisiac.

He took Karen to her car. On the way she said: 'Your boss man – Ilesy. I'm told he thinks the main aim of policing is to keep innocent, civilian blood off the streets. He wouldn't mind pushers and barons getting hit—'

'He'd love that, is always working towards it, preferably so they're killed, but complicated disablement would do. Disfigurement at least – loss of something facial.'

'Not ordinary people in the crossfire, though.'

'He has his own way of viewing things. Crossfire can definitely be a pain.'

'But, look, if Jason and his mates try to eliminate General Franco and *his* mates, there could be a hot war – will more or less certainly be a hot war – probably crossfire, possibly blood on the streets. These people know about weaponry.'

'Which people?'

'The ones Iles wants dead – from either side.'

She'd left her car outside a little group of shops and a chiropody practice called Jubilant, presumably after that line in the 'mine eyes have seen the glory' hymn – 'be jubilant my feet'. Harpur said: 'You drive away first. I'll wait to find whether another vehicle pops in behind. Mobile on, please, in case I need to tell you. You've got a hands-free set?'

'What if a vehicle does pop in behind?'

'You'll know – we'll know – *they* know you've been talking to me. I might even be able to get an identification.'

'But why would they tail me in the first place?'

'They live with the constant expectation of broken trust. All crook cliques are like it.'

'Which they?'

'People around Jason, I'd say. Maybe Jason himself. They constantly sniff for treason. And do checks for treason.'

'And what do I do if they come after me?'

'We've got to hope they don't.'

'Oh, thanks, I think I could have worked that out for myself,' she said. 'But what do I do if they do come after me?'

'You'd have to think about getting out.'

'Getting out of what?'

'Ditching Jason. Doing a bunk.'

'To?'

'Have you got somewhere you could go? Parents? Siblings? Or would Jason know about these – perhaps he's visited them with you, so, not a bright idea. Is there a good, same-sex friend somewhere, just to get you out of sight for a little while, until you find a permanent bolt-hole?'

'This doesn't add up, does it?' she replied. 'If I don't go home because I've got something tracking me, they'll track me to where I *do* go, won't they?'

Yes, a sharp mind here. 'Go home. Act unafraid. Then, when you spot a chance, get in the Mini again and hop it.'

He knew it was dismally poor, entirely fallible guidance. He lacked anything better. Thank God, he observed no car get into the Mini's slipstream. But, as he'd reminded her, these might be smart experts they were dealing with. Perhaps they'd seen her arrive now in Harpur's vehicle. They'd realize he would be watching. They'd have tactics to beat him, and her. To provide a belated reason for being here he stepped from his car and went into the 'eight-till-late' convenience store and bought some wine. Then he left to meet the children.

During the trip to Arthur Street after judo, Jill said from the back seat: 'Shall I tell you how I see the Karen Lister matter?'

'Probably,' Hazel said.

'This is a woman from one of the gangs, most probably Manse Shale's, or Manse Shale's as was,' Jill said. 'Everyone knows there's trouble in the firms because of those killings and then Manse going drop-out and into holiness. There could be a scrap among Manse's people to decide who takes over. Oh, I heard from kids who buy from his outfit that he named someone to run things, but this someone is someone whose brain goes historical and abroad now and then. Not really good for a business.

'Maybe Karen Lister has a boyfriend, partner, who might be thinking of a grab at the top job, to give some true leadership. So, she's scared for him. Very. She thinks that in any battle he could get hurt or even killed, which is most likely right. Maybe he and his little band would be outnumbered. She hopes to bring some sense to things. She's so scared, she wants Dad to meet him and tell him to lay off, and when Dad tells him to lay off he'll lay off, not because Dad told him to lay off, but because, if Dad tells him to lay off, it shows the plan is not a secret, and that means there can't be no surprise, which is vital in such a plot, as all know. Karen has shopped the boyfriend, or whatever he is.'

'Can't be *any* surprise,' Harpur said. 'Or *can* be no surprise.'

'No, there can't be *any* surprise,' Jill said. 'Yes, there *can* be no surprise. That's the picture, isn't it, Dad? You should feel proud, I suppose, because she comes to you and blows the whole plan. She's a woman who seems to trust you.' Her tone said women of this sort were scarce.

'Matilda Shale was at judo tonight,' Hazel said. 'She comes now and then. It's always been now and then. Laura Cave, the little twit, asked her if she wasn't frightened to be in the Jag with her dad after all that. But Matilda stayed calm. She said why should she be scared? The shooting was done, the job finished.'

'Like the job was to kill their stepmother. That's how it sounded, wasn't it, Haze?' Jill said.

'And the brother by accident,' Hazel said.

'Yes, him by accident, but not their stepmother by accident,' Jill said. 'Nobody would bother her and her dad now. That's what she seemed to say. I thought Matilda was telling us, but without the actual words, that she didn't believe Laurent had it right when he said twat Ralphy laid on the Jag shooting. If Ralph had done this, it would be because Manse was a rival in the trade and should be got rid of. But Ralphy wouldn't have such a reason to arrange for Manse's wife to get it.'

As he expected, neither of the children mentioned Karen Lister to Denise. She was already at 126 after the swimming tutorial when they arrived back, and she'd cleared up the living room. No stain on Karen's cup, luckily, because she hadn't come lipsticked. 'I saw your car parked up near Jubilant, Col,' she said. 'I guessed you'd be doing a bit of shopping on the way to judo, so I didn't stop.'

It sounded as though his car was unoccupied at that time, didn't it? Karen Lister must have gone. 'I wanted to pick up some wine,' Harpur said. 'We'll have a glass later, shall we?'

'Who's into currant loaf?' Denise replied.

'Jill and I needed something before judo,' Hazel said, 'to build strength for the arm locks.'

'And the best china!' Denise said.

'Now and then we show Dad we can be ladylike,' Hazel said. 'The crocks are expensive, and we don't want him to feel it's money wasted as far as we're concerned. He deserves some consideration.'

'Definitely,' Jill said.

'That's really kind,' Denise said. 'Isn't it, Col?

'It's family,' Hazel said.

'They're truly thoughtful girls,' Harpur said. He might have liked to talk to Denise, though, about the visit from Karen Lister: talk to and listen to, for her reactions and advice. But the children had obviously decided it would be risky to mention that Karen had called. Perhaps they judged right. Things had to be kept OK with Denise. The remains of that currant loaf could have brought embarrassments. Hazel had headed them off. She had a strong, practical streak. She'd deftly neutralized the loaf by swiftly claiming she and Jill were the ones who'd fed off it. So, no need to admit Harpur had been entertaining a quite young woman with legs and so on here alone for at least an hour.

Just the same, Harpur ran through in his head the kind of conversation he *might* have had with Denise about Lister. Denise possessed a good, quick but dogged brain, perhaps a match for Karen Lister's.

'*The girlfriend-slash-partner of someone in Manse Shale's firm called because she's worried about him,*' Harpur might have said.

Denise would grow alert. '*Called? On the phone?*'

'*No came here.*'

'*To the house?*'

'*It's in the directory.*'

'*If it was business, why didn't she go to the nick?*'

'*She's got an aversion to police stations. It's not uncommon.*'

'*She just rolled up and knocked the door, set on seeing you personally?*'

'*Not exactly that.*'

'*What then?*'

'*She waited in the street until we came out, on the way to judo. She wouldn't want to be seen knocking the door of a senior cop.*'

'*Seen who by?*'

'*She wondered if she'd been tailed.*'

'*So she puts herself on show pounding the street.*'

'*Yes, she's not always very logical.*'

'*Why would she be tailed?*'

'*I don't think she was.*'

'*But why would she imagine it?*'

'*People in these firms don't believe love for one of their members is the same as loyalty to the outfit. The two different interests can clash.*'

'*So, what's her worry about?*'

'*She thinks he's going to try for control of Manse Shale's company.*'

'*The control has already passed to someone, hasn't it? That's what I heard in college. Quite a few students get their stuff from his team. And lecturers. Shale more or less appointed someone, didn't he? Isn't it a bloke they call General Franco, real name Arlington?*'

'*He calls* himself *General Franco from time to time, and acts the part. That's the guts of the problem.*'

'*Yes?*'

'*The boyfriend doesn't think this new leadership with its mental quirks is able to handle big changes sure to come in the drugs game here.*'

'*And the boyfriend thinks he* could *handle them? But she's not so sure?*'

'*Her worries start before that. She isn't confident he can manage the grab for the top job.*'

'*That's a pretty poor response from a girlfriend, isn't it? Where's the love? Where's the esteem? Where's the lustful complicity? It knocks him, poor bugger.*'

'*It does. But she's shrewd. She could be right.*'

'*A lot of people mix up being cautious with being right. Why does she come to you? Is that part of the shrewdness?*'

'*She wants me to see him and hint I'm aware of the plan. She calculates that if he finds it's known he'll chicken. Coups need confidentiality.*'

'*God, this is sleazy of her, wouldn't you say? And isn't it all very flimsy, Col? She's only guessing he might have a go, and that, if he does have a go, he'll get damaged. So hypothetical. This is figment on figment. And suppose you do go to see him. He'll deduce she's spilled to you, won't he?*'

'*Possibly. All the same, she thinks she's doing what's best.*'

'*Do you?*'

'*Not certain.*'
'*Will you see him?*'
'*Not certain.*'

And he wasn't. He had no official cause to interview Jason. He didn't want to bring retaliation and punishment upon Karen Lister. If the chat with Denise had been real, she'd probably have put her doubts much more forcibly. In his fantasy script he provided some of his own weak quibbles for her to speak – but that's all they sounded like: weak quibbles. Denise didn't go in for quibbles of any category. They were enough to make him undecided, though.

'How's the crawl?' he said.

'Better,' Denise said. 'The coach gave me some really close help.'

'Oh, good.'

'Showed me how to get my left arm going deeper and coordinate more closely with leg rhythm. It was a session very much focused on my legs and thighs.'

'Oh, great.'

'You don't have to get steamed, you know.'

'Steamed?'

'The coach is a woman. Hetero woman.'

'Great,' Harpur said.

'Did you get steamed about it?'

'A bit, yes.'

'Great,' Denise said.

Harpur made some more tea, using the quality cups, saucers and plates again, and he and Denise sat on the chesterfield and finished the currant loaf. But watching Denise eat, he thought for a couple of moments again of Karen Lister's good little teeth as part of a death mask.

EIGHT

That dawn search by low law-thugs at Low Pastures brought big changes to Margaret Ember. Above all, she decided she could not leave Ralph, whatever her plans might have been before. To bolt now with the children would look like the filthiest cowardice, and a vile obsession with Ralph's loot. The police had suddenly turned against him after an epoch of gloriously permitted, endlessly incrementing profits; so, his wife buggers off and leaves him to it, scared of more cop harassment, and scared also that the raid could mean Ralph's chief business would get hammered, and the marvellous money shrink or even stop. This was how her escape would be seen. She couldn't do it. She had to stick with him, help him if she could, support him.

She knew the invasion of their house had really shaken Ralph, not just because of that disgusting episode itself, but because of what it told. It told a lot. It told that the special Iles formula of trade tolerance as payback for street peace had been abruptly shut down. Ralph and his family and his property were treated as any old lag and his family and property might have been treated. Iles said they shouldn't consider the raid as spinning Ralph's drum – to use the gross police lingo: just what it was, though, and, obviously, Iles knew it. His remark had been a poisoned slice of waggery, a contemptuous tease. Ralph would be badly upset. Because of his resemblance to the young Charlton Heston, she knew some thought of him as radiating the dignity and worth of Heston's great, heroic roles: El Cid, Moses, Ben Hur; El Cid especially. He'd realize that for them to learn his fine home had been thoroughly thoroughfared by a four thirty a.m. law posse with a warrant would be an appalling shock, possibly not recoverable from.

Although Margaret saw nearly every bit of these Chuck Heston comparisons as idiotic film flimflam, she knew they counted for Ralph and garrisoned his ramshackle ego. It troubled her that if they ceased to work, his morale and his self-image might collapse. They had always been fragile, despite his showmanship. Yes, she'd heard there were men in the business who'd shared dodgy situations in the past with her husband and who now referred to him as Panicking Ralph, or Panicking Ralphy, nicknames that made him sound like a gibbering dud. She hated this, had to help him prove them mistaken, envious and evil, even if they weren't mistaken; most of all if they weren't mistaken. Who'd want to be linked to a Ralphy wreck? She'd admit there came times when, looking at him in the right half light, she, also, saw El Cid. Or Ben Hur. Hadn't she thought of him like that when that bloody raid on Low Pastures started and she'd been ashamed of her half-formed intention to quit with the kids? It was a privilege to back him, wasn't it? Wasn't it? She needed to witness and have a part in that legendary dignity and worth.

Something else Iles had said during the house search remained stark in her memory: the security difficulties at Low Pastures. An abundance of growth offered cover even in winter for anyone wanting to approach the house and grounds unobserved. She stood with Ralph now in one of the paddocks, watching Venetia and Fay on their Welsh cob ponies practise gymkhana jumps, Venetia riding Jasmine, Fay with Billyboy. Because of Iles, Margaret found her attention kept turning away, though. She had to stare and re-stare towards the strung-out beech copse, the shrubbery and hedges, which stood between Low Pastures and Aspley Farm. She eye-hunted for any kind of unusual movement.

It was still her fears for the two girls that disquieted her most. She worried about Ralph as a target, also, and about herself, but less intensely than for the children. She had locked herself into a kind of tit-for-tat logic: Laurent Shale had been shot, and therefore Ralph Ember's daughters could be, should be, must be, vengeance objects. The fact that Shale's second wife was also shot mattered, but it was Laurent's death that brought Margaret Ember her major terrors. Some people in the business thought Ralph must have masterminded the Sandicott Terrace ambush. She didn't know whether they had it right or not. She found that ultimately it didn't matter. God, this did come as a shock and revelation, though. She was his, he was hers, and they must stay together. Although her fears for their children remained great, the conviction that she must not leave Ralph had become a crucial fraction greater.

But, of course, she would like proof that her worries about retaliation against her daughters were unnecessary, were even foolish. Perhaps Manse Shale, and the successor to Manse Shale, didn't at all believe Ralph had fixed the Jag shooting. They might know who did. Or think they knew. That should be enough. It would take the danger away from the Ember household. When she made that solo trip to Sandicott Terrace and saw the distance – the *lack* of distance – where the two cars must have briefly stood alongside each other, she'd registered acute doubt that Naomi Shale had been killed by mistake, the actual objective, Mansel. She could accept that the boy was probably shot by accident: collateral damage, as the military called it. But would even the most inexperienced and jittery gunman fail to see that this was a woman, not Manse, driving, and open up regardless?

And if, in fact, the shots were meant for Naomi Shale and not her husband, this would surely mean Ralph had no involvement. It might be credible that in the constant, traditional aim for monopoly, Ralph would want Manse removed – on the face of it a friend, but also a massive rival and competitor, with his own menacing lust for monopoly. That kind of motivation could not apply to Naomi. She'd come to Manse and this area from London. Had she brought her own enemies? There'd been rumours saying so, though not generally given much belief. If this attack was private to Naomi, with the death of Laurent only incidental, then there should be no threat to Ralph, herself, Venetia or Fay. Iles's analysis of the unprotected approach to Low Pastures was what she had called it before: only his kind of cruel, alarmist tease.

Margaret and Ralph left the two girls working the ponies and went back towards the house. Although winter was certainly settling in, red, white and yellow roses and dark-blue chrysanthemums bloomed in the flower beds. She'd read somewhere lately that a famous writer, V.S. Naipaul, thought colour in a garden suburban and to be avoided. This sounded rather sweeping and harsh. In any case, nobody could term Low Pastures suburban. It was great-house rural.

Ralph put an arm around Margaret's shoulders as they walked. Perhaps he sensed her anxieties and felt he must comfort her. In fact, his gesture scared her more, almost to the point of throwing up under the pergola. It made him seem so thick-headedly confident, so would-be rock-like and celluloid masterful.

'I'm sorry about the raid and foul intrusion, Maggie,' he said. 'One day, and possibly not very far off, we'll be out of the kind of trade that brought such incivility and downright bullying.'

Yes, he sounded assured and magnificently in control. He obviously didn't mean that Iles and Harpur would wipe out his business. Instead, he hinted that, at a time he chose, and possibly quite soon, he would himself decide to close his trading operations: retire from drugdom to run The Monty as a full-time commitment, and possibly other interests, legitimate interests.

Ralph said: 'I know you were pushed off balance a little witnessing that troop swarm all over Low Pastures, and also having to listen to Iles and his mischief. It will end, I promise.' He gave her an extra squeeze with his arm to underline his grand intentions. She found it silly and binding. He could be such an oafish dreamer. He needed her guidance, while he idiotically thought *he* was guiding *her*. She had to be here to save him from his illusions.

'And did you have a warning they'd invade?' she replied.

Ralph enjoyed a big, noisy laugh. She thought of it as the kind of laugh specialized in by owners of large, historic properties with acres, a squire-type laugh, full, resonant, far beyond a chuckle, not too far off a guffaw. 'That notion really upset Harpur, didn't it?' he said. 'They consider themselves so smart. My remark got through instantly, made them wonder if they were smart at all!'

'*Did* you have a warning?' she said.

'One can't run a firm without information.'

'What else do you hear?'

'Much of it useless. An occasional brilliant insight,' he said.

She wanted the occasional brilliant insight herself. She didn't expect to get it from Ralph. Margaret never really knew what kind of information he was giving her. He could fantasize, as his lunatic ambitions for the club showed. Half his life seemed to be fantasy, not the earning half. Most likely this talk of retirement from drugs commerce was fantasy. Maybe Manse's withdrawal had implanted the idea, though she would have expected the reverse: Mansel's abdication should make the competition against Ralph weaker, with a very fallible learner apparently in charge.

Even though Manse Shale had quit, she didn't think she could go and ask him whether he and his people suspected Ralph of laying on the Sandicott Terrace murders, making him therefore radiantly eligible for reprisals, along with Margaret and the girls. What kind of answers would she get from him, even if he agreed to see her while he still mourned? The search for the truth would have to be subtler than that. She didn't know how to find the new chief executive – the one they called General Franco, actual name Arlington – and wouldn't really expect truth from him, either; perhaps not even sense: she understood he could fantasize better than Ralph, almost enough to get him sectioned.

She did know someone who'd been number three or four in Manse Shale's outfit, Jason Wensley. She knew his partner, Karen Lister, too. Margaret had met and liked them at some Monty function and afterwards chauffeured the pair home because they'd drunk too much. People in the firms avoided what could seem small defiances of the law. They didn't want to antagonize the police at any level. Harmony should be coddled. Even at that time, Margaret had realized it might be useful to know where Karen and Jason lived. Karen had seemed very friendly and open-minded. Margaret hadn't thought it was only the booze. Occasionally, she felt she'd love to talk to someone in the same kind of situation as herself – not criminal, but tied to a man who was. There'd be problems to share, worries to discuss and perhaps diminish, perhaps dispel.

Yes, she'd like to see Karen now, chat to her, put some possibly oblique questions to her, woman to woman. Karen might have picked up something of intentions in the Shale guild; had possibly heard where its members put the blame for Sandicott Terrace. Margaret thought she might feel comfortable trying Karen.

Wednesday evenings in the autumn and winter she went to a Keep Fit class near the city centre. She decided she'd leave that half an hour early so she could call in on Karen and, perhaps, Jason. This was the kind of visit she wouldn't tell Ralph about. It suggested – didn't it? – that she couldn't trust him to tell the truth about Sandicott. She couldn't, but it was unnecessary to make this plain. Margaret wouldn't have to worry about the children if Ralph had no part in the killings, and if Shale and his staff believed this. Obviously, these were not identical points. She rated the second as more important. Perhaps Karen Lister could reassure on that. If she didn't – couldn't – might Margaret have to start thinking again about taking the children away, despite her resolution to do what she could to prop him, even in his stupidities and evasions?

NINE

Harpur wondered whether Karen Lister really understood what Jill had called, in her know-all, read-everything, muckraking way, *omertà*: the holy, crook gospel of buttoned lip. Karen Lister would have heard of it, naturally. She wasn't dim or ignorant. But did she appreciate its strength, feel – actually feel – its power: an imported strength and power, yes, a Mafia concoction, but in play here, too, on this patch? Its purpose was the same as in that native Italian scene, or scenes, if Jill had things right about the Naples variant.

Karen seemed to think it would be safe and effective for Harpur to arrive at the house and announce he'd been tipped-off that Jason meant to wipe out General Franco, but must immediately cancel because, (i) it was known about, (ii) it was dangerous, and (iii) it was against the law, Iles's law or Sir Matthew Upton's. Iles's and Sir Matthew's ideas on the law might vary about drugs policing, but they'd be closer on something like murder, though Iles didn't much mind when villains killed one another.

If Harpur did call at their place, she might be present when he made the declaration and would probably act shocked. Did she think this would fool Jason? She wasn't Dame Dench. *'My God, Jason, it would be an appalling risk. Please, drop the idea. Now, please!'* Although there might be other possible sources for Harpur's information, as he'd told her, she would be the most obvious. Perhaps Karen reckoned she could manage Jason, even if he did suspect. This was what made Harpur fear she didn't really grasp the force of the *omertà* edict. A love-match partnership couldn't compete.

Harpur hesitated to expose her, and expose her for what, after all, was only a series of guesses, not a stack of facts: Jason *might* believe the new hands-on supremo of the firm, Arlington-Franco, lacked boss qualities; *might* feel re-fighting the Spanish Civil War a byway; *might* intend to replace Franco;

might try to do it by force; *might* get hurt or worse in any battle for the leadership. A thick goulash of maybes.

Harpur decided he would not drop in at their house: too direct, too blatantly set up, and set up by Karen. No, he'd take an evening drive around the main dealing district near Valencia Esplanade and the docks and hope to come across Jason on his foreman duties; or perhaps he was higher than that now. The chieftain topic could be slipped in as part of casual chat, not its flagrant only purpose. This seeming casualness would be difficult to phrase – not, for instance, '*Oh, by the way, Jason, I heard you want to kill General Franco*' – but Harpur believed it feasible. Dealers had become used to Iles's relaxed regime, so no longer cleared the district when Harpur or any other officer turned up, though their alarm system would announce he had entered the area.

Karen and Jason had a semi in a spruce district, not all that far from Iles's home in Rougement Place. Pavement dog-shit here would be pedigree. Harpur planned to take a bit of a detour through their street and . . . and what? Check the property hadn't burned down? Make sure their recycling bin was out on the proper date? Not much else would be evident. It struck him as on a par with those senseless subsequent visits he made to Sandicott Terrace, a half-baked reflex, an obsession with place, rather than what had happened in that place. He'd tootle past their house and learn nothing, except it was still there. He went, anyway. The reflexes might be half-baked but were compulsive. He drove slowly and tried to get his brain to unscramble why he gave in to this kind of time-wasting, dumbo saunter.

For once, his brain told him he had no need to be stuck in such palsied nonsense. He could park, get out of the car and ring the doorbell, couldn't he? Where was the snag? Where *exactly* was the snag? He had an answer, of course: safety – Karen Lister's. This visit might put her in peril. But, to counter that, couldn't he do some acting himself? All this assumed Jason was at home. Would he be out working? His file recorded that, like most big-time drugs people, he drove a BMW. Harpur couldn't see it parked near the house, but they had a garage. Suppose Jason *were* there, then: Harpur would tell him that multi-whispers came from top-grade informants, saying he planned something very rough. Top-grade informants did exist, though they hadn't come up with anything on a possible putsch. Harpur might remind him that Iles deplored such potentially bloody moves, the opposite of street peace. Harpur would add he didn't like them himself. Hence the warning. Karen could be kept out of it.

And as a result of the pondering, Harpur gradually came to feel freed up, no longer zombified. He did what his mind had told him was OK: parked, got out of the car and rang the doorbell. The abrupt reversal of tactics recalled for him how Karen had hurried away from Harpur's house, then all at once turned back for that original meeting. Perhaps she and he were both liable to get kicked up the arse and vitalized by second thoughts. Harpur didn't mind taking a lesson from her. Iles often told him he needed to expand his thinking. In a kindlier tone than the Assistant Chief's, Denise occasionally hinted the same. She thought he wasn't by nature dull, but nearly always mentally sort of jet-lagged and frazzled through trying to keep Iles from calamity. Ringing this bell Harpur regarded as character development. He'd ditched the do-nothing ritual, at least for now. The front door lacked the majesty of the one Iles had ridicule-revered at Low Pastures. A kid on a scooter could have ridden right through it without injury.

Karen answered the bell. She looked strained, and perhaps had been crying, but was still a wonderfully beautiful sight. Those strong, high cheekbones stopped any serious slump of her face. She seemed startled to see him. Had he made a mistake, after all, by arriving at the house? Did it frighten and annoy her? She'd wanted him to talk to Jason, but had never said where. Perhaps Harpur's own doubts about the wisdom of calling here had been correct. 'Do you know something?' she said. She asked it as if afraid of the answer. She was tense, apprehensive, her voice shaky.

'Know what?'

'Have you come to tell me something? Have you?'

He saw now why his arrival disturbed her. She thought he had bad news that must be given face-to-face. Telling people bad news face-to-face was a standard police duty. Harpur said: 'You wanted me to have a word with Jason.'

'Oh. I see. That's all?'

'What else?'

'I was afraid you might have heard he's—' She tried to get better control of herself, even tried a smile. It didn't work, or come anywhere near working. At times Harpur would try to sketch in his mind how it must be for a woman like Karen, partnered with a man whose career was almost total murk. All right, people argued about whether the drugs business should be illegal or not, but as things stood supplying remained criminal, and so did many of the saucy side issues of that profession: total evasion of income tax; possible maiming and murder, in defence of a firm's ground and/or to colonize by force someone else's. Karen feared Jason was about to use some of that violence on a seeming workmate, Michael Redvers Arlington, alias General Franco. This scared her enough to ignore the silence rule, spill her worries to a cop, and invite him to abort a supposed master stroke by her lover. She lived on the proceeds from his crooked job, but had limits to what she could put up with. This kind of quandary must be continuous for someone like her, and for someone like Margaret Ember.

'Jason's not here,' she said. She didn't ask Harpur in but stood back, as if to invite him.

'Well, he'll be selling or overseeing somewhere. I'll look for him,' Harpur said. So, it was back to plan A. 'That is, if you still want me to speak to him.'

Her position seemed to Harpur very like Margaret Ember's, in fact. Margaret and her children had a wonderfully stately existence behind a magnificently solid front door thanks mainly to Ralph's ardent trade in the substances, but Margaret had at least once, a little while ago, felt she couldn't accept any longer a life paid for by villainy, even cop-tolerated villainy. Like Karen Lister, Margaret had come to Harpur with her anxieties and, in Margaret Ember's case, had actually left home, though not for very long.

'You've heard nothing?' Karen asked.

'What should I have heard?'

'People would report to you, wouldn't they?'

'Which people?'

'Your people, police.'

'Report what?'

'If there'd been anything.'

'If there'd been what?'

'An incident.'

'Which?'

'He should be here,' she said. 'We were eating in. I've been to Tesco.'

They went into a dining room at the rear of the house. There were shopping bags on the table. The floor was close-carpeted in plain beige. A couple of half full red-wine bottles stood on a low, pale-wood sideboard. Four dining chairs matched the sideboard. The walls were emulsioned off-white. There were no pictures. Neither of them sat down.

'You went to Tesco and came back expecting him to be here?' Harpur said. 'Was he at home when you left?'

She nodded. 'I asked the neighbours.'

'What?'

'If they'd seen him go out. God, they must think I'm in a panic attack.'

Harpur would half agree.

'They told me some people had come for him in a car,' she said.

'He went with them?'

'Two men.'

'Went willingly?'

'It wasn't the kind of thing I'd like to ask, was it? These are our next doors. We have to live here. It wouldn't sound good if I suggested he'd been muscled into a vehicle, abducted. What sort of people would they think us – to have acquaintances like that?'

She wanted the household to be respected. Margaret Ember possibly longed for something of the same at Low Pastures. Lately, Harpur's daughter Hazel had been studying a play at school called *Juno and the Paycock*, by an Irish writer. One of its points, according to Hazel, was that the women characters all seemed to have more sense and sensitiveness than the men, particularly the one called 'the Paycock' because of his crazy vanity and showiness. Hazel considered this a very fair glimpse of the difference between the sexes, and so did her teacher, apparently – a woman, of course. Harpur would admit to himself that Karen Lister and Margaret Ember might show more wisdom than their mates, but possibly less moneymaking skill. Denise could be wise, too, although so young, and the nicotine seemed to ginger up her brain and give her extra clarity. Occasionally, or more often, Harpur thought about taking up ciggies himself now Megan could no longer nag him.

Karen said: 'The neighbours didn't suggest Jason was forced. They thought the three must be off on a stag night out somewhere. That makes it all sound cheery, doesn't it? People see what they'd like to see.'

'Did they say what car?'

'Just a car. One of them had happened to glance from the front window. They weren't anticipating anything unusual. They wouldn't bother about the kind of car. Jason went into the back with one of the men. The other drove.'

'You didn't ask?'

'Again, I'm trying to act normal. This is an ordinary evening in an ordinary street. Or ought to be.'

'You didn't get a description of the men?'

'I couldn't ask for that, either. I'd have sounded scared. I *was* scared. *Am* scared. But I wouldn't let on to them.'

'I wondered if you might have recognized the pair from what your neighbours said.'

'They just mentioned two men.'

'If they assumed a stag night, the men would most likely be around Jason's age, I suppose,' Harpur said.

'I don't know.'

'So, you didn't ask them much beyond whether they'd seen Jason?'

'A simple question, not pursued. I acted puzzled, slightly puzzled – said he should have been here, which he should have been.'

'Had he said anything about going out? About a stag night?'

'No.'

'He might have spoken of it a while ago and you've forgotten,' Harpur said.

'No.'

'Do the neighbours know his trade?'

'They know he's in sales.'

'Yes, that's what he's in, flogging the commodities. I was going to have a drift around the Esplanade area,' Harpur said. 'I will now. I imagine there's been a rota change, and he was needed. That kind of staffing emergency. The two might be his team for tonight. Nothing much to it. You've tried his mobile?'

'Voicemail only. I've asked him to call. He doesn't much like using it.'

'No, some people don't.'

'His sort of people, you mean?'

'People in that type of specialized commerce. Mobiles are insecure. All phones are insecure, mobiles most. Anyway, it might be better for me to meet him away from your home,' Harpur said. 'This was my first idea. It makes things more plausible.'

'I'll come with you.'

'That wouldn't be clever, Karen.'

'Why? I want to find him.'

'You arriving with me in my car? It announces where the information came from, doesn't it? Others might see, as well as Jason. Yes, it would broadcast. Crazy, I'm afraid.'

'Please.'

'Stay here and I'll keep in touch. I've got the number.'

'You could put me down on the edge of the district. I'd help with the search. We could stay linked by mobile phones.'

'Best for you not to be walking around alone there,' Harpur said, and meant it. Perhaps those people in Sandicott Terrace were right when they complained the police had lost control of the streets. Iles hadn't objected to the charge. Hell, even the Chief Inspector of Constabulary – Britain's topmost cop – said so a little while ago. There'd been terrible headlines about his findings, and not only in the forever snotty Lefty Press.

Something weird, something glaringly illogical hit Harpur – something *anti*-logical: for no reason he could pinpoint, he

thought the plainness of this room and the dreary paleness of
the wood helped him back off from regarding Karen as, above
everything else, brilliantly exciting sexually. Instead, he saw
her only as a young woman who had turned to the police for
help, and who *should* be helped if he could manage it. He
was able to place the urgencies of the job uncontested up front,
and not those other urgencies which could niggle and arouse
when a man and woman were together unscheduled in an
otherwise empty house.

He felt damn proud of this onset of maturity at last. His
daughters might have been surprised and pleased. The room
said domesticity, and suffered from a beige-ish, wishy-washy,
absolute lack of oomph. He gladly inhaled this disenchanted
atmosphere as possibly one way to get desire nicely and offi-
cially deep dungeoned, on a temporary basis. It had no place
now. Good God, there could be a genuine crisis here: Jason
picked up by a pair of General Franco's people – perhaps
including the General himself – because there had been other
leaks about an insurgent plot, and this was the pre-emptive,
preventive, wipe-out strike. Such a conspiracy would be hard
to keep confidential, and might produce a bevy of rumours.
Clearly Karen sensed this. To call her reaction a panic attack
was probably unfair. Panic attacks might have no evident cause.
Her present fears had a very definite, clear cause. The General
was the kind of successful soldier who'd have built into him
a determination to make the first strike.

'Please take me with you,' she said.

But he looked at that bloody foul sideboard and gratefully
used the sight to push him towards flintiness. 'No, I'll work
faster alone,' he said.

'I don't see that.'

Neither did Harpur, but he needed an exit line. 'I know the
district.'

'All right, so you can show it to me.'

'But when I showed it to you I'd be showing others that
you were with me.'

He drove towards Valencia Esplanade and the tangle of side
streets off it. He was in an unmarked Mazda from the police

pool. After a couple of miles, when he routinely checked his mirror, he thought he saw Karen's blue Mini three or four cars back, maybe with only a driver in it, her. He went on and did a lot of rear-view watching. The Mini seemed to stay for about another mile, and then, as he crossed the Valencia's frontier, it disappeared. Perhaps he had been wrong. There'd be other blue Minis, wouldn't there? He'd love to be wrong. He'd never had a clear view of the car or driver because of vehicles between. Or possibly she'd done her own version of what she'd suggested earlier: left her car at the edge of the Valencia and started a search for Jason on foot.

He rang their house and got the answerphone. He didn't talk to it. He should have taken her mobile number, but hadn't wanted to ask anything that suggested they'd trawl together for her man. How the hell could she have thought that possible? Fright and near-despair must have shut half her brain down. She certainly had one.

He cruised around the Valencia – along the Esplanade itself and through the other, smaller streets. He saw plenty of pushers, and plenty of customers, but not Jason, and not Karen, either. Of course, Jason might be in the Nexus or one of the other clubs. He could be at work aboard *The Eton Boating Song*, a beautiful, ex-China clipper, now a bar and restaurant moored in Spencer's Dock at the far end of the Esplanade: a select clientele – academics, media folk, major villains between chokey spells, company executives, soccer agents, Health Service chiefs, airline pilots. It was the only vessel in the dock. Shipping business had dwindled since those days when the Valencia district got its name to mark good trade with Spain. On the land side of the Esplanade were large Victorian houses, once occupied by merchants, chandlers, ship owners, sea captains. Now, they had been converted into flats, were dilapidated and scruffy, and probably due to be demolished and replaced when local authority budgets perked up, or if.

Harpur parked on some waste ground from where he could watch *The Eton Boating Song* and Nexus and most of the Esplanade. It was a busy evening, very busy for so early. Jason ought to be here somewhere cashing in with his assistants – if Jason was all right. People liked to come down to the Valencia from other, chicer parts of the city for their clubbing and dealing and, perhaps, girling; and they came from outside the city, too. It made them feel undaunted and worldly, bordering on louche. They arrived looking for what he'd heard one classy *E.B.S.* client describe as 'frissons'. Apparently, the Valencia gave frissons by the bucketful. This could be a dangerous spot. Of course it could, or Harpur wouldn't be sitting here searching for at least Jason, and possibly Karen.

Iles's cherished street tranquillity did not always operate in the Valencia. There were freelance, maverick traders unaware of the unspoken, sanctified agreement with Iles to avoid violence, or who were aware of it but didn't give a shit. East European and other immigrant dealers sometimes tried to establish themselves in the Valencia. They couldn't be expected to acknowledge and respect a blessed covenant with the Assistant Chief. They were used to fighting for what they wanted and for what they meant to hold, such as parts of the Valencia, for instance. Big volley battles could suddenly flare, and quieter acts of injury or death, too. So, where was Jason, and, maybe, Karen?

Harpur saw a couple of men, both late twenties, early thirties, approaching the Mazda, one smiling towards him with terrific mock fondness. Harpur recognized Michael Redvers Arlington, Manse Shale's chosen successor as managing director of his firm, who sometimes thought of himself as General Franco and planned the bombing of Guernica. A little behind him, in due bodyguard style, walked Edison L. Whitehead, a long-time heavy in the firm, famous for the quality of his mercy – dead low. Whitehead wore a dark overcoat, almost reaching his ankles, with reinforcing shoulder flaps. Harpur thought it a style copied from nineteenth-century coachmen, and capacious enough to conceal quite serious weaponry. Whitehead had a plump, broad, unlined face that could easily be mistaken for genial. This was one of his outstanding assets. It could beguile enemies – new enemies who didn't know him. His mouth was wide and his lips full. You would expect something hearty from them.

Arlington had on a much shorter tan overcoat. It would have been right for a cavalry officer when cavalry still meant horses.

He had a glistening white cutaway collar and a very subdued tie, dark green with ochre flecks. He was fair, light-skinned with pretty-boy features, not at all like pictures Harpur had seen of Franco. It must be a soul matter, this transformation now and then from Arlington, the drug pusher, to the ruthless Nationalist soldier. Arlington would not let himself get hemmed in by the merely fleshly.

Harpur had the driver's side window already down. Arlington came alongside and bent to speak, leaning against the door. His voice did a lot of first-class affability. 'Mr Harpur, Mr Harpur – Edison was just saying how satisfied you must be to gaze out on the scene here, so animated, so positive, so magnificently civil and friendly. And how has this been achieved? By the enlightened efforts of Mr Iles and yourself, despite opposition.'

Behind Arlington, Edison Whitehead said, 'Visionaries, both of you, Mr Harpur.'

'We know it is Mr Iles who provided the original intellectual impetus for these charming conditions, but I say intellectual-spinterlectual, you have your part, also,' Arlington commented. 'Detective Chief Super Harpur is the one who day-to-day, night-to-night, *applies* this intellectual impetus, makes it, as it were, work.'

'A fine combination,' Whitehead said. 'As near to unique as makes no difference.' Yes, he sounded hearty.

'We regard it as very much your entitlement to come to the Valencia, take a vantage point, and enjoy the sight of a brilliant theory actually in operation,' Arlington said. 'Who, I ask, deserves this treat more than you?'

'We don't consider it vanity that you should motor to the Valencia and view what you've helped create,' Whitehead said. 'This is natural satisfaction. True, there is a pride element present, but what is termed "proper pride", a phrase my dad liked when referring to polished shoes, nicely brushed hair, my pullover free from Marmite stains. This is quite different from arrant, boastful pride.'

'Who's around tonight?' Harpur replied.

'You're right, an exceptionally booming evening for midweek,' Arlington said.

'Did you need reinforcements?' Harpur said.

'Many a more conventional business would crave this kind of take-up,' Arlington said.

'I'm not sure I understand the command structure in your outfit any longer,' Harpur replied. 'Manse is nominal chairman, you come in as MD and chief exec, Michael, but who's your deputy? You might be gunned down tomorrow. Then where are we, for heaven's sake? Someone must be there, groomed, ready to pop in and pick up the tiller.'

'Not me,' Whitehead said. 'You can believe it. I'm never one for the admin side. Doesn't grab me. I like to be out there dealing with specifics. And there's no shortage of those.'

'Edison is famed for that,' Arlington said. 'Well, I suppose you knew already. Speak Edison's name almost anywhere, even abroad, or on luxury cruise ships, and people will respond with: "Ah, he's an unparalleled man for specifics," or the equivalent in their own lingo.'

'Give me a specific to deal with and I'll feel at home and comfortable,' Whitehead said. 'This could be seen as a narrowness in me, but I'd prefer to count it as focused strength.'

'And, clearly, Edison is the sort I need beside me when I tackle this damned anarchist, Commie, atheistic, republican rabble government in Madrid, the so-called "Popular Front", with its fucking intrusive Lefty Brit sympathizers,' Arlington said. 'The International Brigade, spouting socialist junk. Have you heard of the Trotskyist George Orwell, so-called? That's not his real name. He's here. I hate people who give themselves false labels. I'm damn proud of my own name – Francisco Franco – and would never change. Orwell's real name was Blair, so you can see he might want to get rid of it.'

'In your kind of operation, a good aide is invaluable,' Harpur replied. He admired the seamlessness of what had just gone on: this greased move from being Michael Redvers Arlington to becoming an army commander and prospective head of state, and then back to shaping up as M.R. Arlington again, presumably.

'Admin is certainly necessary for our sales programme here and in other local areas, but it's simply not my flair,' Whitehead said.

He obviously took the identity switches of Arlington as normal, and the Franco aspects as ignorable. Perhaps Manse Shale had regarded it in the same way. He saw exceptional big talent in Arlington and might feel a bit of fantasy didn't matter. And so the advancement, not to dictator or general, but to hands-on captain of a notable firm. In fact, Manse might see Arlington's flexible ego as a plus in business. Did it prove he could bring an unrestricted, inventive mind to things? He had originality. He had scope. In history he had found a pattern of unstoppable leadership, which could be useful now. Or, at least, Manse might imagine so in his present off-balance state. Possibly he looked with special kindness these days on make-believe. After all, what had actuality done for his wife and son? Actuality was broken glass, blood and bullets.

Arlington said: 'All right, I'm just a general now, but we'll see where I end up when this thing is over. I've got international friends you know, Harpur. No names, no complications. But these are people of tremendous status and immense resolve. Perhaps, without indiscretion, I might be allowed to mention a swastika. Two words from me and they're here in support. Have you heard the title *El Caudillo* at all, meaning honcho, and undisputed ruler?'

'It's Spanish, isn't it?' Harpur said. 'Suits the Valencia.'

'Of course it's fucking Spanish,' Arlington said. 'What else would it fucking be in Spain? I'll march on them and win that lofty post, or my name's not Francisco Franco, which it definitely and immovably is. Are you with us, Harpur? There's no ducking out. You've got to choose. Forget the failed coup I was part of. This time I'll triumph. Join us!'

'Coups are tricky, wherever they're tried,' Harpur said.

Edison Whitehead said: 'Talking of caudillos, we saw yours chatting to one of the young ethnic girls up near Stave Street when we did another small tour earlier today, Mr Harpur.'

'Desmond Iles?' Harpur asked.

'No, not Mr Iles,' Whitehead said. 'Not the *Assistant* Chief. The Chief himself.'

'Sir Matthew?' Harpur said. 'You sure?'

'This is the girl Mr Iles is very fond of, called Honorée,

but on this occasion it was Sir Matthew Upton in considerable discussion with her,' Arlington said.

'He went with her? Sir Matthew?' Harpur said.

Arlington moved swiftly around the front of the Mazda, opened the passenger door and climbed in alongside Harpur. He sat down and closed the door. 'Some confidentiality required at this point,' he said. 'In all our interests, Edison can listen in from where I was standing myself, but we don't want some of these other folk eavesdropping, do we?'

'I'll disperse them, should they gather,' Whitehead said. 'That's the kind of problem I'm made for. Dispersals, riddings, exclusions – these are my long suits.'

'No, the Chief hadn't come for the usual kind of service from the girl,' Arlington said, 'though she is a stunner, and testament to Mr Iles's taste and staying power. We wondered if Sir Matt was asking her about Mr Iles – sort of building a dossier against him, listing repeated intimacies with one of these purchasable sweethearts. Some would regard it as not fitting for a married Assistant Chief, even on a patch like this. We heard Sir Matthew thinks Mr Iles has been making a total monkey of him – that pre-warned search up at Ralphy Ember's shack. Would Upton be out to get him, do you think? We have a clash of two philosophies, don't we?'

'Sir Matthew is still comparatively new here. It will take him a while to acclimatize,' Harpur said. 'Mr Iles would like to help him, in that way he has with Chiefs.'

'He drove the previous one half bonkers, didn't he?' Arlington said.

'Iles and Upton are going to be at each other's throats, aren't they?' Whitehead said. 'This, also, is the kind of specific that interests me, engages my mind – people at each other's throats. It's a figure of speech, yes, but throats are so real.' He put a hand in through the window and touched Harpur's. 'There's a distinct physical nature to throats. Vital, or they wouldn't be up to swallowing.'

'Upton will try to eliminate the firms, won't he, Mr Harpur?' Arlington said. 'He rejects the ACC's happy, enlightened theory of cooperation between him and us. Why I spoke of a clash of philosophies. This could be grave. This could be wider than is immediately apparent. We have to ask whether Sir Matthew has been given the Chiefship here by some Home Office mogul specifically to obliterate the trade and its traders.'

'*Specifically*,' Whitehead said. 'Yes, that would be another specific I can understand and attempt to deal with – Upton sent here with particular orders to do a total clean-up. He's already a knight. He'll be after a peerage for purification.'

'Starting with the raid on Ralphy,' Arlington said. 'They're looking for something that would pin the Shale murders on to Ember. If they can take him out, the firm goes under.'

'This would explain the Chief's rage with Iles who, in his view, sabotaged at Low Pastures the first move in the campaign, by giving Ralph the tip it was due, and, therefore, time to remove anything unhelpful,' Whitehead said. 'It's very obvious.'

Arlington's face glowed, and he sat up straighter to invoke militarism. '"Campaign" is a word I'm very *au fait* with,' he said. 'Youngest general at thirty-four, not just in Spain but in Europe. It would be neglectful of me not to mention this. Battles in Morocco, next against a miners' revolt in Asturias, and then the start of this Civil War in '36. I think I can reasonably claim to be an expert in campaigns, although, as a matter of fact, my dad wanted me to go in the navy!'

'And after Upton had done for Ember's outfit he would turn on us, thinking we must be weak on account of Mansel's disappearance,' Whitehead said.

Arlington bellowed an exceptionally full, contemptuous laugh. 'Weakness is hardly a characteristic to be associated with someone who made it to general at that age, I think. How does it strike you, Mr Harpur?'

'Did you get any of the conversation between Upton and the girl?' Harpur replied.

'The Chief's not going to ask *you* to dig out bad information about Mr Iles, is he?' Arlington said. 'Sir Matthew would regard C. Harpur as one of the ACC's cabinet, and as someone who feels penitent and indebted towards him, because of that lengthy lewdness with his wife in various locations, often listed by him. Nor could he reveal to other detectives that he's trying to destroy his own Assistant Chief.

It would look decidedly poor form. So he has to corner the girl himself.'

'Did money pass?' Harpur said. 'They don't like standing around gossiping unpaid. Tricks could be missed.'

'In a way it's brave of Upton,' Arlington said. 'He must be very determined. Still daylight at the time. There are many CCTV cameras. I hope he knows how to keep his face private. As a matter of fact, I took a couple of crafty shots on the mobile myself. For the record.'

'As I've said, my own view of the Shale firm's leadership structure now is Manse as a sort of president-patron, you as the working main man, Michael, then Jason Wensley,' Harpur replied. 'That right?'

'I hope Sir Matthew won't have you banging on my front door one morning at four thirty a.m.,' Arlington said.

'Is Jason working tonight?' Harpur said. 'Both of you doing supervision? Did he have to be, as it were, drafted in?'

'There's certainly a lot of customer demand to satisfy,' Arlington said. He opened the passenger door and swung out of the car. 'You've reminded me I should be visiting the rest of the ground. Thanks for that, Mr Harpur.'

'Don't you divide the overseeing rôle with Jason?' Harpur said.

'Some would maintain this district has taken a tumble socially,' Edison Whitehead said. 'Yet there is a fine liveliness present. We do not need to forget the distinguished maritime history. But it has been succeeded by a change of purpose. It has been inevitably brought up to date. We and you and Mr Iles are commendable parts of that progress, Mr Harpur.'

They strolled away, Edison taking a standard, two-steps-behind guardian position. *El Caudillo* had lived and ruled into his eighties and must also have had efficient protection. This pair's car would be just around the corner from here, in Templar Street. They had an established, well-known procedure for visits to the Valencia. They used three parking spots in turn. They'd leave the car and do a kind of walkabout, checking on their people working that patch, some of them inside one of the clubs or pubs or on the *Eton*. Then they'd move on by car and stop in Mill Place, and, lastly, Gladstone Square, and

do similar foot patrols and visits there – another pub and
Morgan's caff. Apparently, General Franco liked the regularity
of this, thought it helped make the firm look reliable and
organized, like an army unit. The obviousness didn't matter,
because their trade was tolerated. In fact, he possibly saw the
obviousness as a plus – part of that reliability. And nobody
would be stupid enough, suicidal enough, to vandalize or nick
their car. Now they would go to Testament Place before their
last call at Gladstone Square. You could imagine it had all
been expertly planned by the team who choreographed royal
weddings and the state opening of Parliament.

Harpur, himself, took another slow drive through the
Valencia, this time looking for not only Jason and Karen, but
possibly Upton and Honorée, as well. He saw none of them.
He phoned Karen's and Jason's home again and got the
recording once more. He found himself gripped by that useless
urge to see their street and house, not simply make mobile
calls, and in a while he returned to Carteret Drive and parked
at a distance from the semi. It was still in darkness. He decided
to wait. He couldn't have explained why, and resented the slip
back into automatism.

TEN

As she'd promised herself, Margaret Ember finished the Keep Fit session half an hour early. She showered and dressed, then set out for the house of Karen Lister and Jason Wensley in Carteret Drive. She'd driven them there that night after they'd had too much at a Monty do. Her clothes were more formal than she'd usually wear for her Keep Fit visits. She had on full-heel black patent shoes, a dark suit and crimson blouse under an all-wool, black, knee-length winter coat. She wanted Karen to realize that this was an important, special call. She wouldn't mention she'd tacked it on to the curtailed gym trip. It would sound like an afterthought. She'd like Karen to feel flattered that Margaret had taken obvious care with her turnout for this meeting. It might help things along.

To arrive unannounced at their semi was a gamble. She hoped Karen would be there alone. Most street and club trading went on in the evenings, and Jason should be out marshalling the sales people. Margaret knew she'd have to get very delicate with her questions if Jason should be at home. Well, not questions, plural – one central question: was a hit-back attack on Ralph and his family planned by the reshaped Shale company? He might refuse to answer. He might laugh the question away as outrageous and barmy. Or he might answer with lies. How would she know what *was* the truth? Did it seem conceivable that a member of one firm would disclose the outfit's plans to the wife of another firm's head?

Margaret believed Karen would be more sympathetic, more likely to feel moved by possible danger to the children. Perhaps she had picked up hints of what the company's attitude was towards the Shale deaths. Possibly, she could offer some reassurance – supposing, that is, there was reason for reassurance. If not, Margaret would have to think again about making a run from Ralph with the two girls. The insult and insolence

of that police raid on Low Pastures had made her determined
to side with him and abandon any thought of quitting. What
was that corny song – 'Stand by Your Man'? She'd felt it a
necessity then. But now concern for their daughters came to
dominate her thinking again. The responsibility gripped her.
She found she couldn't believe in the competence of Ralph
and his people to guard them. How *could* they be efficiently
guarded when they had to go on with their normal lives? Only
absence could properly guarantee their safety – and her own,
though this did not rank as a major item with her.

The house in Carteret Drive seemed completely dark, but
she parked and walked through the small front garden and
rang the bell. Did she sense someone move in the front room
of the neighbouring house, move furtively, sticking to the
shadows, in case of being noticed? The curtains there were
not closed, and the lights out. She had no response to the bell
and rang again. She waited. She heard a door open in the
house next door. An elderly woman, burly, round-faced, good-
tempered looking behind slightly ornate spectacles, appeared
in the porch there. She said: 'Excuse me, but they're not at
home. I hope I'm not interfering, but there's been quite a bit
of what has to be termed "activity" there tonight, so we've
been keeping an eye. Not nosing, you understand – we hate
that kind of behaviour – but it's unusual for them to have so
many visitors, of very various kinds. Frank and I wondered
whether there's anything wrong. We're very fond of Karen.
And then there's Jason, also. A nice quiet couple, usually. I'd
be sad if anything had happened to Karen. Anything unfortunate, that is.'

'No, nothing wrong. I'm a friend. I thought I'd drop in.
What kind of activity?'

A man joined the neighbour in their doorway. He'd be about
her age, mid-seventies, a little stooped, bald, thin, with a
meagre grey moustache, watery but cheerful eyes.

'I've been telling this lady there's been rather a lot of activity
next door tonight, Frank.'

'Activity is the word!' he said.

'Yes, activity,' Beryl said.

'We both came upon that term to describe things, quite

separately from each other. Beryl said to me, "Such a lot of activity next door, Frank." And I had been going to say more or less the same to her, such as, "There seems to be ongoing activity next door tonight, Beryl." I don't mean noisy or trouble-some in other ways—'

'Not at all,' Beryl said.

'But activity. Noticeable activity. I don't want you to think we're peering from the front windows all the time, prying,' Frank said. He gazed both ways along Carteret Drive.

'Not at all,' Beryl said. 'I've explained that.'

'But we couldn't help noticing when a car arrived,' Frank said. 'I happened to have stepped into the front room and was about to put the light on when I heard and saw the car pull up. The curtains were not closed. We don't use the front room very much. I had gone there looking for the atlas, to do with Mount Kilimanjaro, in Tanzania, which our grandchild, Amy, is doing a sponsored climb on, one of its peaks being the highest in Africa, its snows the subject of a film with Ava Gardner. Amy's a tough one, will have a go at—'

'Who was in the car?' Margaret said.

'I didn't switch the lights on,' Frank said. 'I thought at first the vehicle had stopped outside *our* house. I was curious, as I think you'll agree is natural, but didn't want to seem to be staring, which would have been the case if I went to the window with the lights on behind me. So, I didn't bother about the atlas for the moment but moved into the middle of the room and looked at the car.'

'Oh, and before this,' Beryl said, 'I had seen Karen drive off in her blue Mini, which was quite usual on some evenings, when she goes to Tesco for the shopping. She leaves her car outside, but his is an expensive job and kept in their garage. Then, later, I wondered what Frank was doing, spending so long looking for the atlas, but no lights on, which would have shone into the hall, and I'd have been aware of, so I went into the front room, and he said about the car. We both watched, because this didn't seem usual in the way Karen going to Tesco was usual. Often she'll ask me if she can get anything for us there. She's *so* helpful. This type of kindness is not always shown by young people these days.'

'Who was in the car?' Margaret replied.

'Two men at first,' Frank said.

'They went to the front door and rang the bell,' Beryl said. 'There were lights on in the house, so we knew Jason must be there, most likely.'

'Excuse me asking, but are you to do with the men in the car?' Frank said. 'We don't mean to be hounding you with questions, but there does seem to be something . . . something, well, *unusual* about such a string of people coming to their house tonight.'

'A string?' Margaret replied.

'This car and the men were only the first. That's why I referred to "ongoing",' Frank said. 'And then there might be someone hanging about outside, not necessarily coming to the house on this occasion, but interested in the house.'

'Oh?' Beryl said. 'I didn't know that.'

'Watching?' Margaret said.

'That's how it seems,' Frank said.

'Did you recognize the men in the car, I wonder?' Margaret said.

'Strangers,' Beryl said. 'That's one reason it all seemed so . . . well, *unusual*. We didn't refer to it at that time as "activity" because so far this was the solitary unusual aspect, and not *very* unusual, anyway. It was only two men in a car calling on them. Obviously, they might just be friends of Jason. I considered it would be over-egging to call it activity.'

'Or ordinary household business, such as measuring up for fitted carpets or double glazing, which might have required two people,' Frank said. 'Yes, it would have been an exaggeration at that stage – at that stage – to refer to the car and the men as activity.'

'Yes, I see,' Margaret said.

Frank had a lengthy chuckle. She felt his lungs seemed well up to it.

'What?' Beryl said.

'Well, this lady is herself part of the activity now, isn't she?' Frank said. 'We're discussing the activity with somebody who is a part of that activity! This makes it quite a remarkable development, in my view. Sort of circular.'

'What were they like, the two men?' Margaret said.

'It was dark, of course,' Frank said.

'But even so, you'd get some impression,' Margaret said.

'Frank thought late twenties both,' Beryl said. 'I'd say one late twenties, the other older, perhaps thirty-two, even thirty-five. Jason is most probably in that age group – say between twenty-eight and thirty-three or four, so it could have been mates calling for him. We didn't discuss this at the time because things seemed quite ordinary, as we said. But later, when we began to think of it all as activity, we tried to remember what the men were like. This was to do with searching for an explanation for the activity, but only later when we'd come to the conclusion that what was going on had to be described as "activity".'

'They got out of the car and went up to the front door, just like you did,' Frank said.

'Could you get a look at the faces when they were nearer, in the front garden?' Margaret said.

'The thing is, we had to stand well back in our room or they might have seen us and thought we were having a snoop,' Frank said.

'Which we were,' Beryl said. She giggled.

'Well, yes, but only because we were concerned about Karen,' Frank said.

'Right,' Beryl said.

'Very understandable,' Margaret replied.

'We're discussing all this with you since you have become an element in the activity, you see, and perhaps you'll be able to work out what's been happening,' Frank said. 'You might see a pattern in it, on account of information you have, not available to us. You come at matters from a different angle.'

'Soon, the two men, plus Jason, left the house and climbed into the car,' Beryl said.

'How did they seem?' Margaret said.

'In which respect?' Frank said.

'When they went to the car,' Margaret said.

'Karen asked us that,' Beryl said. 'This is a sort of crux?'

'You've spoken to her?' Margaret asked. 'That would be when she'd come back from Tesco, would it?'

'She came back and found the house empty because Jason had gone with the two men,' Beryl said.

'Jason in the rear with one of them and the other driving,' Frank said.

'What I meant was, did he appear to go willingly?' Margaret replied. 'Or did he look scared, try to resist?'

'I had an idea Karen wanted to ask us that, but she couldn't because she wouldn't like us to think they knew people who might come for Jason when she was out and make him go with them,' Frank said. 'This is quite a good area, and I know Karen was very keen to fit in.'

'Coming for someone in a car and trucking him off – it would be like one of those crime films,' Beryl said. 'There's that old, grim phrase, isn't there, to "take someone for a ride", meaning the someone is not coming back, owing to a fusillade, most probably in some secluded rural spot.'

'It's not the kind of thing you expect to happen in Carteret Drive,' Frank said. 'But that's how people always comment, isn't it – e.g., on TV news when police start digging up bodies in someone's back garden? Local people want the audience to realize it's not happening all the time in their district, discovery of multi remains under a private lawn. They always remark they're "devastated" by that type of discovery in their neighbourhood, though not as devastated as the victims being dug up.'

'We saw Karen return from Tesco and carry her shopping inside,' Beryl said. 'I think Jason had left some lights on, so she would not realize until then that he'd gone. She most probably checked their garage and saw his car still there. After a few minutes she came around and rang our bell and asked if we'd seen him go. She had never done anything like that before. We told her about the callers.'

'This is when we both began to think of what was going on as activity, although we didn't realize at the time that the other one had also decided on that word,' Frank said.

'At first, I didn't like it very much,' Beryl said.

'What?' Margaret said.

'Karen coming to ask. As though she thought we were always secretly watching what went on outside,' Beryl said.

'Sort of spying. In a way it was cheek, like, assuming we'd have been in the front room observing because we did a lot of it. We *had* been in the front room observing, yes, but she shouldn't have guessed that.' There was a low fence and some shrubs between Margaret and them, and the division seemed to stop Beryl and Frank from asking her into their home.

'But then Beryl came to understand there might be something strange going on tonight,' Frank said. 'We could see Karen was really bothered, though she pretended something different – like, acting casual, sort of amused by the mystery of it, such as where had he skipped off to, the naughty boy?'

'It didn't work,' Beryl said. 'She wouldn't have come to us like that unless she was really worried; her face tense – mouth screwed up tight, breathing rather difficult. You'll know the signs. Well, anyway, we couldn't help more than that – speak of the car and the two men – and she went back to her own place to wait for Jason, maybe ring around to where he might have gone.'

'And then, what was definitely a matter of "activity" happened,' Frank said.

'Who do you imagine arrives and rings at the mauve front-door next?' Beryl asked.

'Who?' Margaret said.

'Beryl *thinks* it was,' Frank said.

'Who?' Margaret said.

'I've seen his picture in the media after that shooting in Sandicott Terrace, the woman and boy,' Beryl said. 'This is a police officer, though not in uniform. He's the kind who wears plain clothes.'

'A detective,' Margaret said.

'This is one of the chief detectives,' Beryl said. 'Chief Superintendent, or something of the sort.'

'If she's right,' Frank said.

'What did he look like?' Margaret said.

'Do you know anything about boxing?' Frank replied.

'Not much,' Margaret said.

'It's a long way back, anyway,' Frank said. 'There was a world champion called Rocky Marciano. American. This one looks like him, but fair-haired, not dark like Marciano.'

'Harpur?' Margaret said.

'You know him?' Beryl asked.

'Are you police yourself, then?' Frank said. 'I wondered – the smart way you're dressed and the questions.'

'I've heard some describe Harpur as like some boxer, but with fair hair,' Margaret replied.

'Do you know people who talk about the police a lot then?' Beryl said.

'It came up in conversation once or twice,' Margaret said.

'In which regard?' Frank said.

'And he went into the house?' Margaret replied.

'We counted the time. He was there for twenty minutes,' Frank said. 'Then he drove away. But before his car disappeared, Karen came from the house, jumped into the Mini and seemed to go after him. I think you'll see now why we considered all these events very puzzling and exceptional.'

'And then, bless us, *you* arrive,' Beryl said. 'No wonder that by this time we're calling it activity. We'd really appreciate it if you can tell us what's happening. It seems to me we have a right to know, being close neighbours who might possibly be involved in some . . . well, in some situation.'

'I think he's out there now,' Frank said.

'Who?' Margaret said.

'The one like Marciano, but not altogether,' Frank said. 'Although he's parked quite a way off, I believe it's him.'

'You didn't say, Frank,' Beryl said.

'I mentioned a watcher. But I don't want you frightened, particularly as I'm not sure,' Frank said.

'How would it be frightening?' Beryl replied.

'Why would he be there now?' Margaret said.

'I was hoping *you* could tell *us*,' Frank said.

Margaret looked up Carteret Drive. 'Which car?'

'The black one,' Frank said.

'The Mazda?'

'I'm not good on cars,' Frank said.

'Excuse me, but are you *acting* surprised now?' Beryl asked Margaret. 'You knew he was there, did you?'

'Are you police?' Frank said. 'Is this an operation?'

'Has something happened to them – Karen or Jason, or both?' Beryl said.

Margaret's car was facing away from the Mazda. When she left Beryl and Frank, she thought of turning, so as to get close enough for an examination of the driver as she passed, but decided this would tell him he'd been spotted, if it actually was Harpur. It might be best he didn't know that.

ELEVEN

From his Mazda parked in Carteret Drive, Harpur had watched as a red Lexus convertible coupé, about sixty grand's worth, passed him and pulled up near number eleven, the Lister-Wensley house. He routinely noted the registration number of every vehicle that moved along Carteret Drive in either direction. He'd seen this car before, anyway. It had stood on the Low Pastures forecourt alongside Ralph Ember's Bentley during that early morning call sponsored and later wholly mistrusted by the Chief. Now, Margaret Ember stepped out of the Lexus, walked the few steps to number eleven, went through the front garden and put out a hand to ring the bell. Although Harpur was a long way from her, he thought she seemed very formally and elegantly dressed. The house remained in darkness. The blue Mini was absent.

Margaret stood waiting in the porch and raised her hand again, apparently to try another ring. Harpur saw an elderly woman come out from the house next door and begin to talk to her over the fence and shrubs. Soon, a man of around the same age as the woman appeared from behind her and joined the conversation. They must have seen and heard Margaret's arrival from their front room. It was not lit or curtained. They'd probably be on high alert tonight. Had they decided to do their observing in secret? There must have been several callers – the two men in the car, mentioned by Karen, and, of course, Harpur himself. The neighbours might have recognized him as police: he got some television and Press publicity during big cases. If they did, it would stoke their edginess. Then the departures: those two men plus Jason, the relationship between the three uncertain, possibly rough-house; later Harpur would leave, and then Karen, probably. Now came this other visitor in the glossy car, Margaret Ember.

Harpur tried to work out why she would be calling here. The neighbours must be doing the same, he thought. Margaret's clothes suggested this was an important visit. Harpur failed to get much beyond that bit of guesswork, though. He didn't even understand how Margaret could be on visiting terms with these people. Their links were with a different firm. He wondered whether the neighbours had found out anything from her. The talk appeared quite intense for most of the time. But at one point the man turned away briefly and gazed up and down Carteret Drive. Did his eyes stay an extra second on the Mazda and Harpur? He would need 20-20 vision. Harpur was in the back of the vehicle. If you were watching somewhere from a car you used the rear seat, not the driver's, where you'd be more plainly on show, and where people would expect you to be. The distance from numbers eleven and thirteen ought to make the Mazda look unoccupied.

After about a quarter of an hour Margaret moved away from the house and got into her Lexus. For a couple of moments, Harpur feared she would do a U-turn and again pass the Mazda and who was in it, but this time face-on. Perhaps, after all, the oldies had mentioned the possible surveillance to her. Or had she spotted him when passing the Mazda on her arrival? But she drove away out of the other end of the Drive, presumably back home to Low Pastures.

Harpur wished Iles were here. He could be brilliant on people's motivation. This had astonished Harpur when he first witnessed the ACC's gift. After all, Iles's outlook was so enthusiastically, and so vastly, at variance with all normal human impulses, it seemed unlikely he'd understand how others' thinking might work. Harpur attempted to get his own head into the kind of mind-reading state that Iles would apply so effortlessly, if a situation interested him. Occasionally, a situation did. Harpur believed the Assistant Chief would almost certainly want to diagnose Margaret Ember's reasons for coming to Carteret Drive. Harpur wondered if they had anything to do with his own woolly, go-nowhere reflections on the lives of women partnered by villains. Was Margaret here to suggest a female alliance with Karen across the two firms, and to hell with the men? Margaret might have calculated that Jason would be out at work, so she and Karen could talk privately. Did Ralph know his wife had made this trip?

Harpur saw questions and more questions, but no clear answers. Iles would regard that as pathetic, retarded, and fully in character for Harpur. He thought he could recall from Margaret Ember's dossier that she went to a Keep Fit class on Wednesday evenings. Had she come on from there? It would explain why she entered Carteret Drive from one direction and left by the other. If Margaret had quit the class early she could carry out this visit without Ralph knowing, although the smartness of her clothes would possibly have made him curious. People didn't normally dress up for the gym.

Harpur waited. At just before ten o'clock a grey Volvo estate car drove into Carteret Drive and passed him from behind, as the Lexus had. Three men aboard, two in the back? The car stopped outside number eleven, but in the middle of the road, not pulled over to the pavement. Harpur sensed its engine must still be running, though he was too far off to hear. A tall, dark-haired man of about thirty wearing a black leather jacket and jeans got out from the rear seat. Harpur instantly recognized him as Jason Wensley. He seemed to give a thumbs-up sign to the two in the car, then quickly entered the house and closed the front door after him. Some lights came on inside. The Volvo moved away at once and turned left out of Carteret Drive.

Harpur rang in for a trace on its registration. While he was phoning, Karen's Mini passed and she found a parking spot near number eleven. She climbed out of the car, locked it and sprinted to the house. She let herself in. Yes, 'sprinted' was the word: arms pumping, hair flying behind. He thought he could read excitement and joy in this short, vigorous dash. She would have seen the lights in the house and deduced Jason was home. After a few minutes, the couple from next door came out again and stood in their front garden staring up and down Carteret Drive and occasionally at the mauve front door. Then they went back into number thirteen. They might feel the 'activities' were over now and they could relax. The Control Room told Harpur the Volvo had been stolen two days ago in East Stead.

He drove to the Valencia again. Once more he did his slow tour of the Esplanade district, this time looking for General Franco and Edison L. Whitehead, his chaperone. Business in the area had hotted up since he was there an hour or so ago, but he didn't see them on their management duties around the streets. He left the car and tried the Nexus club, and then *The Eton Boating Song*. The thumbs up from Jason to his mates in the Volvo disturbed Harpur. So did the report that the Volvo was stolen. Had he been coming at this problem from the wrong end? Had Karen come at it from the wrong end, too – misjudged who would get to be a victim, victims? The Nexus barman said he hadn't seen Franco tonight.

The Eton Boating Song had been called *Imperial Majesty* when it regularly brought tea from China to Britain in the nineteenth century, but was rechristened for the present role. Its new name lacked supreme majesty, but had a degree of social class, all the same. She was a three-masted vessel with a broad bow raked forward for speed: a clipper had to clip, and what it clipped was voyage time. Harpur thought the ship still looked very businesslike and capable of crossing an ocean or two if they replaced her canvas, though it would be years since she actually spread her square-rigged sails and traded. Some repairs and reconstruction had taken place over the decades to make sure she stayed afloat against the quay, and to accommodate a bar and restaurant and up-to-date plumbing, but the graceful lines of the long hull remained as they'd been when she was launched. She did very good business moored alone in Spencer's Dock. Alongside stood a preserved but unused crane commemorating a time when the port thrived and freighters were loaded and unloaded there daily. People liked a touch of the maritime, a feeling of history.

There were about fifteen customers in the bar, including Honorée. Although management weren't enthusiastic about joy girls using the *Eton*, they tolerated Honorée because she usually dressed modestly and waited for men to pick her up, not the other way about. Also, they might have an idea about her serious, extremely ongoing connection with Iles, and realize how malevolent and unforgiving the ACC could get if he ever felt she, and therefore he, had been slighted. Plus, she was black, and to ban her could appear racist. Tonight she looked lovely, Harpur thought, in a cinch-waisted tan-coloured parka jacket and excellently tailored dark trousers,

her hair cut short and tufty so there were no hanging wisps
to shroud her beautifully composed profile. She had a client
with her, a very thin, hatchet-faced man in his sixties, wearing
a fine, old-style, substantial, green-brown tweed suit that might
have been what held him together. He had on, as well, brogues
and a paisley tie backed by a yellow, tan and dark-red check
shirt. He and Honorée hardly looked made for each other, but
interesting, Harpur thought. He did not see Arlington and
Whitehead, and went to have a glance around the crowded
restaurant, but they weren't there, either. When he returned to
the bar, Honorée gave him a little wave, inviting Harpur to join
her and the punter where they sat on a crimson padded wall-
bench near the door. 'This is Neville, Col,' she said. 'He's
from far away – Preston, or Yeovil, somewhere like that, and
does roofing materials and flagstones, so fascinating.'

Neville shook hands. 'Delighted,' he said.

Harpur sat down next to him.

Honorée leaned across Neville and said: 'They're after
Desy.'

'Yes, I know,' Harpur said.

When she bent forward to speak, the movement started a
thick drift of scent towards Harpur. It seemed of quite reasonable quality. Iles would never give her cheapo stuff, partly
because he'd hate to smell of something inferior himself after
contact. Iles knew a lot about scent and always called it that,
not perfume: 'Ad-man's term,' he'd told Harpur.

'Who's Desy?' Neville said.

'Col knows everything, Nev,' she replied. 'General Franco
and his corporal have been talking to you, have they, Col?
They saw the big Chief with me earlier. I noticed them having
a stare. Photos taken?'

'General Franco?' Neville said.

'I guessed what Upton would want,' Harpur said.

She pulled back and sat very upright, her neat jaw jutting,
warlike: 'Oh, bloody thanks, Col! Are you saying that's *all*
he'd want from me?' she said.

'Was it?' Harpur said.

'Something's gone wrong between the two of them, hasn't
it – Upton and Desy,' she replied.

'They come at things from different angles,' Harpur said.

'The tale around is the Chief thinks Des blew an operation,' she said. 'Like, treachery?'

'Did Upton say that?' Harpur replied.

'It's the word around,' she said.

'What operation?' Neville said.

'You should tell Des about Upton and his scheming,' she said.

'Well, yes,' Harpur said. 'Or *you* should.'

'I don't know when I'll see him. It could be urgent, couldn't it? I'm not allowed to make contact myself. Unprofessional.'

'Who's Des?' Neville said. 'Tell him what?'

'The Chief wanted details,' she said.

'Did you give them?' Harpur said.

'Would I?' she replied. 'He asked about times, locations and whether official vehicles had been used at all, or a spot near the rugby scrum machine in the police sports field.'

'Used for what, or can I deduce? Times and locations as to what, or can I deduce?' Neville said.

'Deduce away, Nev,' she said. 'It can do no harm.'

'Did he make notes?' Harpur said.

'I didn't tell him anything,' she said. 'There were no notes to make.'

'He might have made a note of that,' Harpur said.

'What?' she said.

'That you didn't answer certain questions,' Harpur said.

'I didn't answer *any* of them,' she said.

'This might have told him something,' Harpur said.

'You mean, I told him something by not telling him something?' she said. 'I claimed courtesan-client privilege and said I could only give interviews if my lawyer was present. Lawyers.'

Neville said: 'Might we move on now, Honorée?' He seemed aroused by the word 'courtesan'. Maybe he thought it made him kingly, despite the roofing materials.

'Where did you see General Franco and his mate, Col?' she replied.

'Why?' Harpur said. 'They were on their usual walk from Templar Street.'

'Another tale around. One of the girls had a little whisper from somewhere that they might not be all right,' she said. 'Not ongoing all right.'

'A little whisper from where?' Harpur said.

'You know how it is, Col,' she replied.

'How would he know how it is?' Neville asked.

'Col will know how it is,' she replied.

'"Not be all right" in which way?' Harpur said.

'Yes, in which way, Honorée?' Neville said.

Sometimes Harpur wondered what people from outside made of this domain as they got occasional cloudy glimpses of how it ran, or half-glimpses. Neville was struggling.

'Not all right at all,' she said. 'All right for now, and when they were talking to you and spying on me with the Chief, yes, but not all right soon, unless they're careful.'

'Chief of what?' Neville said. 'A police Chief? Are *you* the police?' he asked Harpur. 'Honorée mentioned the police sports field. Is that a clue?'

'"Unless they're careful" how?' Harpur replied.

'Everyone should be careful,' Neville said.

'You'll be all right with me,' she said. 'Won't he, Col?'

'More than all right,' Harpur said.

'It's quite an area, this,' Neville said.

'We're doing our best with it,' Harpur said.

'Which "we" is that?' Neville said.

'One day, when the country has more money, the district will be changed, I expect,' Honorée said. 'Developers are sure to come and knock down these old houses and put up new ones. Perhaps this is not so very good. Something is going to be lost, and there'll be no work of my sort or some other sorts. Bad. But, yes, some parts of the Valencia are bad already – one or two big houses not fit for people to live in any longer. Empty. They decay. They are unsightly and very dangerous.'

'Dangerous how?' Neville said.

'Yes, dangerous. They're dangerous, aren't they, Col?' She stood and finished her drink. 'You're very patient, Neville.'

The Control Room came through again and said the Volvo estate had been found abandoned in a non-CCTV'd side street a mile and a half from Carteret Drive.

'Your wife calling?' Neville said.

'See you next time you're down from Preston, Nev, with the rafters,' Harpur said. 'We like to make strangers feel they're very welcome.'

'Which "we" is that?' Neville replied.

'Honorée, did you see Jason around at all?' Harpur said. 'Probably with a couple of chums.'

'God, you *do* know everything,' she said.

'But, excuse me, isn't he asking you something because he *doesn't* know it?' Neville said.

'He knows what to ask, though – that's the thing,' she said.

'Is it?' Neville replied.

'But I don't answer,' she said.

'Why not?' Neville said.

'I don't point the finger,' she said.

'*Omertà*,' Harpur said. 'Silence.'

'I've heard of that,' Neville said.

'There's quite a bit of it around here,' Harpur said. 'One lad has it on his gravestone: "Plenty of *omertà* now."'

The two men in the Volvo might have had another vehicle parked somewhere close, and they'd probably transfer to that. Perhaps door-knocking sessions would be necessary: a search for witnesses in the side street who might have noticed an unfamiliar car left there; an unfamiliar car waiting for a switch-over, though the witnesses couldn't have known this.

Honorée and Neville left. Harpur got another lovely scent waft as she passed. He went outside and stood at the ship's rail. He watched them descend the gangplank to one of the waiting taxis. She turned to wave as though he and the *Eton* were just about to sail to China again for a tea refill. There was an odd feature to the wave, though. She kept most of her hand folded down but used her forefinger to indicate something to her right. She continued this gesture for what must have been a good thirty seconds. A signal of some sort? And had there been other disguised signals? Was she seeking to tell him something, without seeming to tell him – because of *omertà* and its iron demands? Her town planner's survey of housing prospects for the Valencia had trundled on for a while, hadn't it? Was a hint contained there? '*Yes, dangerous. They're*

dangerous, aren't they, Col?' Had she wrapped up something
solely for Harpur in this lecturette, not for her client? Neville
could make do with the property chat.

Harpur followed the line her message might suggest. She'd
said she didn't point the finger, but maybe she did offer that
kind of singling out after all. She seemed to mean Gladstone
Square, off the Esplanade, and Arlington-Franco's final calling
station – supposing she meant anything at all. Harpur had an
idea that there were at least a couple of those decaying, disin-
tegrating villas in the Square, too bad even for squatters.

He left the *Eton* and returned to his car, then drove to the
Square. Progress. Progress? Arlington's big silver Chrysler
stood there, lights out, unoccupied and near one of the abandoned houses. Police pool vehicles carried a torch as standard.
He took it and walked to the Chrysler. It was locked. He shone
the beam in and did a slow, careful survey. He saw nothing
to trouble him. He went back to his own car and sat there,
waiting to see whether Franco and Edison would return.
Morgan's café was on the other side of the Square, with The
Porter pub next door but one. They might be in either of those,
or possibly calling on a sales-staffer at home in one of the
still-occupied flatted properties.

Of course, they'd be surprised to see him here. After all, it
was less than two hours since they talked up near Templar
Street. He must avoid implicating Honorée. The Valencia's
magnificent buzz network would report that Harpur had chin-
wagged with her on the *Eton* for a fair while this evening.
Arlington and Whitehead were sure to guess the tip came from
Honorée if Harpur spoke a warning about some unidentified
peril on its way to them. They'd call on her for more facts,
which perhaps she wouldn't want to give. They might then
turn forceful, despite Honorée's link to Iles and his cultivated
capacity for vengeance and simple, unwavering hate.

Harpur needed a less dangerous subject. He decided that
when he re-met them he'd ask about relations with Ralph
Ember, as a kind of postscript to their earlier discussion. For
instance, did Arlington know Ralph? Did he like him? Did he
think he could get on peacefully with him and his people, as
Manse Shale had? Did he intend recognizing all the holy

frontier lines between Ember's trading ground and Shale's? These were questions Harpur would genuinely like answers to. Mainly, though, they were meant to hide his real reason for waiting in Gladstone Square – the warning from Honorée that Arlington, and therefore Whitehead, might be in for trouble. But maybe trouble had already hit them.

He knew he'd probably have to look inside the three totally derelict grey stone houses; or at least one or two of the totally derelict grey stone houses, depending on what he found in the first or second, if anything. And he knew, too, that he was putting this off. He'd do his robotic, probably useless, evasive bit as starters: check the caff and the pub.

He went on foot to scout for them in Morgan's and The Porter. He was beginning to feel like a licensing inspector tonight. Morgan's, nothing. The Porter was a roomy, oak panelled pub. It had once been a ship owner's mansion, with good views out to sea. It still had the views, but the building had begun to show its age. Locals used it, and some people from up town who liked a touch of history and anti-smartness. It was fairly crowded tonight. A group of four men he recognized as mid-list pushers from the Shale companies stood at the bar and quickly made a space for him among them. It must be their evening off. They knew Harpur's usual drink – a double gin topped up with cider in a half pint glass – and Galileo Smith ordered one for him now.

Galileo was about thirty, wearing an army desert camouflage outfit, wide-shouldered, broad-necked. He spoke with solemn delight: 'Mr Harpur! Just the man we need. There's something of a debate going on here. Your opinion would be valuable. You can give a totally different perspective.'

'Different from what?' Harpur said.

'It's bracing to have your kind of mind applied in a setting such as this commonplace pub where the bulk of folk tend to share the same, insular way of regarding things,' Galileo said, with a big, grateful smile.

'Which things?' Harpur said.

'Who do you think was here earlier?' Galileo replied. 'Well, you observe – are trained to it. You're a detective! You'll have spotted the Chrysler. Yes, General Franco with his unbribable sidekick, Edison L. Whitehead. Well now, look, Mr Harpur, Franco is in the firm's topmost job – or the topmost *field* job. Manse is, of course, still the topmost of topmosts, even though he has removed himself from the workaday arena. I would never blame Manse for that, in the awful circumstances. Who could?'

'Where's General Franco now?' Harpur said.

'Routinely, he calls here to see what trade down this end of the ground is doing. That's understandable enough, we don't usually object to an inspection,' Galileo said. 'Around the *Eton* and the Nexus is the only territory where both firms operate together – sort of intermingle – so it's natural Franco wants to make sure matters stay comradely and sweet.'

'Where is he now?' Harpur said.

'I'd go further than stating we don't object,' an elderly, grey-haired, pony-tailed member of the group said. 'We *approve* of his visits. We gain from his visits. He brings a sense of community and of team solidarity.' He wore a very formal, excellently cut, dark-grey double-breasted suit over a high-necked crimson string vest, no shirt, plus a faux-pearl necklace. Harpur could place him as Oswald Venning Garnet.

'Well, yes, yes, we approve if the visits are conducted properly, sensitively,' Galileo said. 'This is not always the case. Tonight it was not the case.'

'In which way?' Harpur said.

'And so the arguments here,' Galileo replied, 'and the welcome prospect of an opinion on the topic from someone such as yourself, Mr Harpur, unbiased and free from fixed ideas.'

'I need to talk to him,' Harpur said.

'We heard you'd already been observed talking to him up near Templar Street,' Alec Charles Geen said. 'Was that dud info, then?'

'Where did it come from?' Harpur said.

'Franco actually in your car, an unmarked Mazda,' Alec replied. 'The two of you in the front; Edison L. Whitehead outside at the open, driver's side window. An impromptu conference.'

'Another matter has emerged since that meeting,' Harpur said.

'Franco and Edison, drinking matily with us, chewing over sales figures, optimum mixture proportions, and future deliveries, is fine,' Galileo said. 'A model of how to run a company and exercise a business plan, given current conditions.'

'And then what do we fucking get?' Alec asked. He was the smallest and frailest looking of the four. He'd be about forty-five, gaunt-faced, sharp-chinned, parchment-pale, perhaps into H.

'Exactly,' Galileo said.

'What?' Harpur said.

'Alec and I are totally put off by it,' Galileo said. 'Vernon here is not sure. Ossie thinks it of little concern, if any at all. And so the debate, Mr Harpur, in some senses healthy – folk demonstrating their freedom of thought – but also, perhaps, harmfully divisive, even destabilizing.'

'These very small, very occasional, very brief moves away from the normal don't really affect the main situation,' Oswald said. 'Ultimately, Michael Arlington is Michael Arlington. That's my point, Mr Harpur. I don't want to go on about it, but that's my point. The firm is healthy, as healthy as it has ever been, including when Manse was in totally effective control. I hope I would never speak of Manse with disrespect, but Arlington has shown there are various kinds of effective leadership. It's why I say he is ultimately what he is, i.e., himself.'

'How ultimately is ultimately?' Galileo said.

'I'll tell you what we fucking get,' Alec said. It was as though he hadn't heard any of the intervening talk, and now moved in on his own juicy question. His voice boomed hugely; astonishing from that skinny frame. H habit or not, no wonder he'd become emaciated: he put so much of his substance into getting heard. But he'd be easy to pick up and chuck out if the landlord thought him too noisy. He'd hit the pavement with a rattle of bones like a bunch of chopsticks. 'What we suddenly get, tacked on to a wholesome, wise trade causerie, is the big, triumphalist declaration from Franco that he and his chum, General Emilio Mola, are stoutly holding Seville and Granada in the south, and Galicia, Navarre and most of old Castile in the north. "Viva!" he yells. Naturally, it's not

General Mola who's with him but Edison L. Whitehead, attendant in chief. Edison is completely unembarrassed by all the ancient Spanish shit. He just gazes around the bar, no expression on his brute mug. I believe he doesn't even try to look like Mola. OK, I've never seen pictures of Mola but I'd bet he didn't resemble Edison. Yet Edison is indifferent to this lack of verisimilitude. He pretends Arlington-morphed-into-Franco is not happening and that everything's just as it should be. And Oswald here is impressed and agrees, and maybe Vernon does, too.'

'Franco talks of a new aircraft unit, the Condor Legion, organized by German advisers and formed to help him against the Popular Front,' Galileo said. 'Tonight, in here, he orders two bottles of Veuve Clicquot to celebrate. He asks at first for a magnum, which is probably what generals do when they're feeling uppish, but, come on, is a pub like this going to stock magnums? The toast was, "To the glorious wings of the condor!"'

'We all got a drop in a flute, but that's not the point, is it?' Alec said. 'What we're in danger of, because of Arlington's delusions, is a vacuum and people wanting to fill it.'

'Nature doesn't care for vacuums,' Harpur said.

'Manse goes and leaves a big space alongside Ralphy Ember,' Alec said, then abruptly stopped. 'No, no.' His voice swelled even further, as if he needed the extra to drown and correct what he had just said. 'It's not a vacuum. Not a vacuum at all. General Franco's in there, isn't he?'

'Where is he now?' Harpur replied.

'He's worse than a vacuum,' Alec replied. 'He lives on make-believe and shadows and history. The people wanting the territory don't. He can be blown out of the way like a deadhead dandelion. And when he's blown out of the way we are, too, whether it's by Ralphy or some firm from outside.'

'I'm sure you can see the nature of our disagreements, Mr Harpur,' Galileo Smith said.

'You heard of the Peter Principle at all, Harpur?' Alec said.

'Did Franco mention where his next call would be?' Harpur said.

'The Peter Principle is well known,' Alec said.

'I'm certain Alec doesn't mean you suffer from it, Mr Harpur,' Vernon said.

'The Peter Principle is to do with managers,' Alec said. 'It states that people are promoted to one step above what they can handle, and so there's catastrophe. Think of Gordon Brown. Think of Chamberlain. Think of Franco. That's *our* Franco, not the real one. The actual caudillo hung on to the position till he died, and he'd most likely say, "Stuff the Peter Principle. Take a peep at yours truly," but translated into Spanish.'

'The question is, will *our* Franco take us to catastrophe, Mr Harpur?' Galileo said. 'We need your analysis.'

'Have you seen any other people from the firm around tonight?' Harpur replied. He bought drinks, not Veuve Clicquot, but beers for Oswald and Galileo, a rum and black for Alec, rosé for Vernon, and Harpur's own brain-clearing cocktail.

'Which people?' Alec said.

'Or do any of the firm work from one of the flats here?' Harpur said. 'Would he and Edison be going to call on somebody there?'

'You can see our dilemma, Mr Harpur,' Galileo Smith replied.

'But perhaps Mr Harpur doesn't, doesn't in the least see it, because there's no sensible grounds for calling it a dilemma,' Oswald Garnet said. 'We all have our little quirks and fancies. They don't interfere with our work. I instance the Queen with those foul corgis, yet she still does her Parliament spiel OK. I'd like us to consider Alec's reactions in rather more detail than we have heretofore. His phrase, you'll recall, was: "And then what do we fucking get?" I believe I'm quoting him correctly. I want to focus on two crucial words there. I wonder if any of you can nominate which.'

Harpur said: 'So, let's try for a narrative, please: you drink the champagne and clink glasses for the toast, which must have been the culmination of the visit. Did Franco give any indication of where he would be making for afterwards?'

'Of course, the words I want to focus on in Alec's question are "and then",' Oswald replied. '"*And then* what do we fucking get?" Alec asked. What, I would in my turn ask, does that vital "and then" suggest?'

'Franco's movements after the little Civil War ceremony here could be of real significance,' Harpur said.

'Clearly the "and then", in Alec's rather hostile question, means that something has gone before,' Oswald said. 'This is what the then-ness of then is all about, isn't it – something following something else? So, let's examine what preceded Alec's "and then". What preceded it was, as described by Galileo, the excellent company talk concerning sale figures, mixture proportions, deliveries and, above all, a suitable business plan for the current situation. We note that Galileo rated these proceedings as "fine", even though Galileo is not well disposed towards Arlington. I would agree with Galileo's comment on those initial discussions. In fact, I go further than "fine". They were excellent. They proved how brilliantly perceptive Manse was in spotting Mike Arlington's talents and rewarding them with the chief exec post.

'I'd like to point you towards that business plan Galileo spoke of. The trading conditions for the future on this patch are not easy to predict. A credible plan has to be both flexible and clear. For example, tonight, we have the advantage of Mr Harpur's presence at our deliberations. But will this happy cooperativeness continue? It is part of a civilized ambience established and cultivated by Mr Iles. However, we know, don't we, that a new Chief has taken over, and a Chief who does not see the commercial scene in the same positive, healthy fashion as Mr Iles. There is likely to be a power struggle and, despite Mr Iles's high-quality grey matter and filthy ruthlessness, Sir Matthew Upton might prevail. Goodbye then to this constructive socializing with Mr Harpur. He would have to abide by Upton's dictates.'

'Iles was able to fuck up the Low Pastures search ordered by Upton, wasn't he?' Vernon said. 'That's the word around. Do we really think anyone can beat Desmond Iles?'

'We have to cover all possibilities,' Oswald Garnet said. 'And the prospectus that Michael Arlington outlined to us this evening expertly does that. Every contingency, every subdivision of a contingency, was admirably dealt with. Could anyone else in the firm offer that degree of skill? Mansel obviously didn't think so. Neither do I. Jason Wensley? Jason might kid himself he could, but I believe all of us here would deeply doubt it.'

'True,' Vernon said.

'We go back to Alec's "and then",' Oswald said. 'And then, yes . . . and then, after that brilliant exposition, Michael Arlington suddenly switches to game-playing. He feels entitled to relax. He drops into fantasy. His mind soars, has no cramping, restrictive boundaries. This is a positive aspect of the make-believe Alec referred to. Shouldn't we all see – all, including him and Galileo, possibly Vernon – that this ability springs from the same originality which enables him to visualize – and prepare for – each uncertainty of our marketing future? Alec's "and then" was spoken in a tone suggesting a contradiction exists between Michael Arlington's professional intelligence and his excursions into a distant, military past. They are not. They are both integral to one magnificently gifted, uniquely creative person.'

'You know, I find myself coming around to Ossie's opinion,' Vernon said confidingly.

'That's because you're a full-time fucking bejewelled jerk,' Alec replied, at volume max.

'Except I'm forty per cent up on your miserable sodding sales return for the quarter,' Vernon said. He went into a silent, very thorough and long-drawn-out laugh at Alec's rubbishy trading performance, alleged. Vernon was black, getting fat, and in jogging trousers and a navy polo-necked jersey. He wore Lennon-type, rimless glasses and had a small, imperial beard under his lower lip. Harpur thought Vernon's dossier gave his birth date as 1976 and named a wife and three children. 'No fucking offence meant, Alec, you hopeless fucking tit,' Vernon added warmly.

'You can see the situation is unsettling for us, Mr Harpur,' Galileo said. 'A certain very unfortunate edginess and harmful vocab. I wonder whether you have a comment or two to restore confidence, reinstate that previous splendid fellow-feeling among us.'

Harpur downed his gin and cider. 'I have to look about,' he said.

Alec said: 'Harpur, I heard you were on the *Eton* earlier, talking to the Assistant Chief's friend, Honorée.'

'How?' Harpur said.

'How what?' Alec replied.

'How did you hear it?' Harpur said.

'Did you find out what Sir Matthew Upton had been saying to her during quite a long interview, I'm told?' Alec said.

'Who told you?' Harpur said.

'But we can guess his mission, can't we?' Alec replied. 'He's building a case against Iles. He's building a case to destroy Iles. This Assistant Chief uses a girl who spreads herself for money all over the area and will go with someone who deals in roof slates. It could harm Iles, and I don't mean infection only. Repute. Character. How will the Home Office view that sort of behaviour in a very senior married officer, a father? You can see why I'm troubled, and why Galileo is troubled, and Ossie and Vernon would be troubled too if they had the merest fucking brainpower.

'We've got two kinds of threat to our careers in the substances vocation. There's Michael Arlington and his whimsy, which leaves him and us liable to extinction. And then this other possible extinction – Iles. If he's terminated and Upton installs the regime he fancies, we're nowhere.' Alec slowed and stopped. His thin little face twitched five or six times and didn't seem able to reassemble itself into how it had been previously, unpleasant but stable. He began to weep, obviously battered by double despair. He did not attempt to hide his distress – didn't lower his head or moderate the din level from what it was when he spoke. The sobbing hullabaloo reached all parts of the bar. Customers stared, some sympathetically, Harpur thought. 'Oh God, oh God, how have we allowed this situation to come upon us?' Alec asked. 'Shall we see the annihilation of this beautiful, impeccable system, so lovingly formed and maintained? Are we the prey of vandals?'

Oswald Garnet moved to Alec's side and put an arm around his flimsy shoulders. 'We are, perhaps, at opposing points in this argument,' Oswald said, 'but friendship and empathy can still prevail.'

'Take the twattish twerp outside, Os, and give him a good shaking,' Vernon said.

'I forgive you that harshness, Vern,' Alec said. 'We are all stress-affected.' He turned to Harpur. 'Some think me flinty and abrasive. But I have emotions. I can suffer. *Did* Honorée confirm Upton's purpose to you?'

'You're all sure Franco and Whitehead didn't hint at what they'd be doing after The Porter?' Harpur replied.

'Why so anxious?' Vernon said.

Yes, why? These two were low-life, not worth fretting over, surely. It must be Karen Lister's possible involvement via Jason that unsettled him. He didn't want her dragged into something rough, perhaps rougher than rough. He reckoned he had a duty to her. Hadn't she risked coming to him at home in Arthur Street for help? The children were present for part of it. They'd regarded her as a sexual danger, but they would also expect Harpur to do all he could for her. Non-sexually, that is. He had an unexpected vision again of her death mask and the small teeth.

Harpur hoped that when he left the pub the Chrysler would have disappeared from its spot in the Square and he could assume Arlington and Edison L. Whitehead were somewhere about the Valencia on their usual, routine business programme, encouraging, checking, replenishing: this was a commercial enterprise that could not run itself; it required dedicated and energetic, inspired leadership. But, as he came out of The Porter, he saw at once that the Chrysler still stood there. He thought, though, it might not be in exactly the previous position, but possibly a couple of metres forward. Another difference, and maybe more significant: the car was no longer unoccupied. Edison L. Whitehead sat behind the wheel. He seemed to be alone in the Chrysler. It remained unlit. Edison's head moved continually, left, ahead, right, behind, then left again, as though he were looking for somebody and had started to panic at their continued absence.

Harpur walked to the car. Edison lowered the driver's window. Harpur bent forward and leant in. 'It's like a re-run of that earlier conversation up near Templar,' Harpur said. 'But it's me outside this time and you in. And Mike Arlington was present then. Where is he, Edison?'

'I'm waiting for him, as a matter of fact.' He seemed to try to make it sound light and casual. It didn't. The words came without a stumble, though.

'Where is he?' Harpur said.

'He'll be here soon.'

'Where is he?'

'This is a sort of regular rendezvous point for us if we have to separate occasionally.'

'What's happened?' Harpur said.

'He'll be along.'

'You've left him on his own?'

The question obviously knocked Whitehead hard, and he couldn't answer at once. Then he said: 'But he'll be here soon.'

'Should he walk solo in the middle of the night in the Valencia?'

'No, of course he fucking shouldn't,' Edison said. The words were still well managed, but they arrived in a rush now, as though he couldn't act calm any longer, or keep his fears bottled.

'What's happened?' Harpur replied.

'I told him.'

'What?'

'That as head of a firm he shouldn't go unprotected here. I said Manse wouldn't have. It's not a matter of cowardice. Basic caution. But you know how Mike can be.'

'No, how can he be?'

'Well, like, imperious.'

Edison had an education and a vocabulary. Harpur said: 'The General Franco stuff?'

'I'd prefer not to discuss it,' Edison said.

'Sometimes it's best to talk about these things.'

'Which things?'

'If they're troubling you.'

'Well, yes, they're troubling me. I expect you can tell.'

'I'll get in the car. More re-run.' Harpur went around to the passenger door and let himself in. 'It's troubling you that he hasn't turned up, is it?'

'It's not like him. Well, *some* of it's not like him.'

'The lateness?'

'He ought to be here.'

'Which of it *is* like him?' Harpur replied.

'You know how he can be.'

'The Franco stuff?'

'We were over in The Porter early in the evening.'

'Yes.'

'You've been there tonight?'

'Yes.'

'Well, it was all going fine at first.'

'Trade talk.'

'Exactly. Good, sensible trade talk. Nobody can beat Mike at that. He'd asked for four of our people to be there for a bit of a meeting. They could skip street work tonight. We had replacements out – good, industrious replacements, eager to get a feel of the territory, map the trading points.'

'I hear he's great at business surveys,' Harpur said.

'A true talent. Onassis wouldn't be in his league.'

'Gifted.'

'Wonderfully.' Edison shifted in his seat, turned his head half right suddenly to look out of the driver's side window. A man had crossed the Square near Morgan's. Edison must have thought it was Arlington. But, no. He slumped back. 'Was that little sod Alec Geen still there when you went to the pub tonight?' he asked.

'He broke down.'

'Broke down why?'

'He thinks the whole fabric will get ripped to bits.'

'Fabric? Which fabric?' Now, Whitehead stared directly forward through the windscreen, as if expecting to see some of this fabric flap and billow in the breeze off the sea.

'The commercial arrangements,' Harpur said.

'Oh, *that* fabric.'

'The confab in the pub turned awkward, did it?' Harpur said.

'Awkward? Maybe that's the word. It will do, anyway. At a certain stage, as always, no pause between sense and lunacy, we started to get Granada and Seville and Navarre and all that holy insurgency crap from Michael, plus a town called Huesca this time, which I'd heard of. In the north. Orwell served there. Got shot in the throat near Huesca, I think.'

'He was a well-known writer, wasn't he?'

'Michael laughed and laughed, sort of satirical, because some enemy general said, "Tomorrow we'll have coffee in Huesca," but his army never took the town from the Nationalists. Look, Mr Harpur, I've had to work out a way to deal with these fits. I try and act as if they're not happening. That's my usual. But I can see this Geen is in a fucking rage. Anyone could tell he thinks Michael is just a prime liability who could sink everybody. Maybe one of the others does, too – Galileo Smith – but milder, more reasonable, though definitely not happy with Mike. OK, OK, we've been through this kind of situation before, often before. My job? My job is to play it indifferent, which I do. That's to say, in their presence I do. Some harm has been done, though – harm to Mike, his image in the firm. It's plain. Ossie Garnet might be OK, and maybe Vernon. Only maybe. The other two, not at all. Garnet – he's older and doesn't want to be older. So, the ponytail, meant to proclaim plentiful locks, and not grey. Plus, on the psychological side, the urge to be positive, to seem open-minded, progressive, a youth in outlook.'

'This Spanish excursion upset you?'

'Mike's a wonderful guy, in many aspects a near-genius. Would Manse Shale have picked him otherwise?'

'But there are lapses?'

'We were going on from the pub to see a couple of our people in the flats. He's all right with them. Not a mention or even a hint of Seville and the fucking Huesca coffee – non-coffee. When we're coming away, I mention to him in the nicest way you can imagine, Mr Harpur, that these meetings in the flats were absolutely great – so I'm giving him the positives first – but I added that the Civil War thing could get staff irritated, unfortunately. Example? Geen and Smith in the pub. I said they couldn't see the relevance of these journeys into the past.'

'And he reacted badly, did he?' Harpur said.

'He jumps on that one word.'

'Which?'

'"Relevance." He asks, "Relevance to what?"'

'This was a big and idiotic mistake on my part, Mr Harpur.

I could see that at once. I'd have liked to ignore it and go on
to something else. But I had to stick with it now.'

'With "relevance"?'

'He asks again, "Relevance to what?" I know the way his
mind's going. There will be hellishness.'

'I'd have thought it quite reasonable to say people like Geen
and Smith grew tired of the unreal, didn't see where it fitted
in, and therefore regarded the extra, imagined, battlefield role
of Arlington as irrelevant, though interesting and extremely
well-researched.'

'Well, yes, it might be reasonable, Mr Harpur, but we're
not in the realm of the reasonable, are we? This is fairyland.
"Relevance to what?" he inquired once more. He can be like
this when he's F.Fing as I think of it – Francisco Francoing:
hostile, ruthless, determined. And I had to go ahead with it,
didn't I? Unwise to defy F.F.'

'He's not Francisco Franco.'

'*Very* unwise to defy him,' Edison replied. 'I said, "Relevant
to now."

'"I see," he said, "to now. I see. *Now*. And, pray, what is
now?" He'll do this "pray" ploy when he's pissed off, turn on
the hoity-toit, *de haut en fucking bas*.

'I said – again in a fully considerate tone – "Now is here
in the Square, Michael, The Porter, the Valencia."

'"Valencia?" He snarled it. "Full of Commie and Trotsky
shit. That city strives against me. You wish to ally yourself
with them? You, allegedly so close to me, so trusted by me
– you wish to ally yourself with *them*?"

'Of course, I'd felt him going Spanish again. The "now" he
was living in was "then" – the Civil War – at least for now,
as it were. I'd noted the swaggering and the haughty way with
his head, like "show me an enemy and I'll bury him for the
sake of my beloved country".'

'Right.'

'The beloved country being Spain, of course.'

'Yes, I think I got that,' Harpur said.

'I don't really want to discuss this, Mr Harpur. It doesn't
seem . . . doesn't seem . . . doesn't seem appropriate. It's
disloyal to a great man, great intermittently.'

'Suddenly, and for the moment, *you'd* become the enemy? Is that it, Edison?'

Briefly then Harpur thought he might have to deal with another convulsively weeping man. Edison's breathing became very shallow and rapid. He put a hand up to his face, perhaps to brush a tear away, or to check whether there *were* tears on his cheeks. The hand and arm shook a little. His face was square, his features rugged, but, as with Geen, grief or frustration or pain, or all of them mixed, brought rampant skew-whiffness to his looks.

Whitehead said: 'He grew aggressive, asking why I was trying to pass myself off as his friend, General Emilio Mola, killed in an air crash, even though I didn't in the least look like him. "Fraud! Charlatan! Conspirator!" he yelled. We were in the street. People could hear him getting shrill – the way Mr Iles does with you sometimes, because of his wife. They were watching, some giggling. He screamed denials that he'd fixed the plane crash so there'd be no rivals for the caudillo job. Of course, I'd never said anything about the plane crash. I'd never heard of it. He thinks I'm claiming to be Mola's ghost, come back for vengeance. As you'd expect, I wanted to get Michael to the car, make things private. But he looks at the Chrysler and doesn't recognize it. No, it's more than that. He behaves as if it's not there. He's Franco, isn't he, and they didn't have that brand new Chrysler model in the 1930s, not even in the late 1930s. He says he'll walk.'

'Walk where?' Harpur said.

'He's done this kind of thing before. There's some tale that Franco led a big march in tough conditions when he was stationed in Spanish Morocco. Mike wants to get in his foot-steps. Recreate his footsteps.'

'So he wanders alone into the Valencia?' Harpur said.

'Not wanders. He goes at fast infantry pace. It's meant to show disgust with me. He wants distance between us. He sees me as someone out to corrupt the military and undermine the blessed cause.'

Again he seemed close to sobbing. 'What time was this?' Harpur said.

'Is that important?'

'It might be.'

'About nine o'clock.'

'You talked to me near Templar Street at around eight.'

'Yes. Then we went to The Porter and to the two flats. It would be about an hour, perhaps five minutes more. Trade talk, Spanish talk, champagne in the pub, then a bit more trade talk at the flats, not completed, but good. He bought champagne in The Porter to celebrate getting his own air squadron. I think maybe he jumbles up Civil War dates. It's a farrago. Sometimes, the Civil War is over and he's *El Caudillo*. He was on the other day about some Spanish film director called Berlanga, or like that, who makes subtle fun of him in his movies. He said, "Berlanga is not a Communist, he is worse, he is a bad Spaniard." And then that time-shift business with the Orwell-Blair name.'

'You haven't seen him since just after nine?'

'He usually comes back pretty soon. The morph episode ends, and he's Michael Redvers Arlington again. I sat in the car and waited. When he didn't show, I drove around the Valencia looking for him.'

'You were worried?'

'Not badly then. He could be anywhere, not necessarily on the streets – in a club or a girl's room. I went to that black girl's place – the one Mr Iles is fond of. I've often driven Michael there and picked him up afterwards. He likes the notion of sharing her with an ACC, a sort of nice conviviality. But she wasn't there.'

'Tonight, she's with a pleasant chap called Neville, from somewhere distant. You must have missed her. You've tried Arlington's mobile?'

'Switched off. I keep returning to the Square, expecting Michael to be waiting there. No.'

'He could have come back to what you called this rendez-vous point any time while you were away searching other parts of the Valencia, couldn't he?' Harpur said.

'He could have. But if he did, he'd be here waiting for me on the pavement when I returned from one of these sweeps.'

'Maybe,' Harpur said. 'I passed the car at about eleven fifteen on my way to Morgan's and The Porter, and it was empty.'

'I hoofed it to the flats in case he'd got fed up waiting in the Square and had gone to see one of those people again. There was still some business to finish with both of them. But, again, nothing. I made one more tour in the Chrysler, and then came and parked here again. And now you've appeared, but not Michael. I don't know what to do, Mr Harpur.' Once more it seemed as though he'd come apart, mouth open, his prize fighter's chin hanging loose.

Harpur did some chronology. He'd watched Jason Wensley in Carteret Drive leave the stolen estate car at about ten o'clock, and saw him give his pals a thumbs-up goodbye. Arlington had been loose and alone in the Valencia from about nine. If he'd got over his Franco spell and returned to the Square, Edison and the Chrysler might not have been there, because they were somewhere trawling for him. Possibly, Arlington-Franco was alone and non-protected near the wrecked houses at any point after he'd soldiered off from Edison and the car. There'd be time. Did Arlington normally go armed? Harpur couldn't recall anything from the dossier about weapons.

'I suppose a lot of people would know you often used that spot in the Square for the car when you came on calls to Morgan's and the pub and flats,' Harpur said.

'It's not a secret. Mike hates furtiveness. That's not a quality he'd associate with F.F.'

'He's not F.F., nor even F.,' Harpur said.

'Just the same.'

'What's that mean?'

Edison went silent for a while. Then he said: 'I listen to the direction of your questions, Mr Harpur.' He tightened up his face and now made himself sound controlled and purposeful.

'I'm trying to get the pattern of the evening,' Harpur said.

'You think he came back when I wasn't here?'

'It has to be possible, Edison.'

'I was wrong to go hunting for him?'

'It's a natural thing to do. You couldn't know how long he'd remain Franco and continue the great African march, or linger with a girl. The length of that march would be its most important characteristic for him. He'd want to give duration to it. You're certainly not to be blamed.'

'Blamed for what?'

'I had a tip something might have happened over here in the Square,' Harpur replied.

'What tip?'

'Or less than a tip, I suppose. A sort of momentary signal.'

'Who from?'

'Information zooms around the Valencia, doesn't it?' Harpur said.

'Someone saw something here?'

'Someone may have seen something and then mobilephoned it to a friend.'

'Which friend?'

'This is speculation,' Harpur said.

'But you did get the signal?'

'A kind of signal, yes.'

'Which kind?'

A signal half enclosed and hidden in a wave because Honorée thought it should be kept confidential from Neville. 'Nothing very specific,' Harpur said.

'I'm happiest with specifics.'

'I've got a torch in my car. I'm going to have a look in these empty houses.'

'Look for what? Michael wouldn't go in to dumps like these.'

'No, I don't suppose he would.'

Another silence for a while. Edison must be trying to picture Harpur's scenario. 'So you think someone saw an incident to do with Michael and these houses?' he asked.

'I'm guessing.'

'What kind of incident?'

'It would obviously be something that the onlooker thought unusual enough to call about, if I'm guessing right.'

'A struggle?'

'It could be.'

'And there might be several others involved?'

'Could be.'

'You mean taken into one of these houses not of his own accord? Forced? Like an abduction? And this was witnessed and described on a mobile to someone – the someone who gave you the vague signal?'

'That kind of thing.'

'Why wouldn't the witness do something to help?'

'We're in the Valencia,' Harpur said.

'Who's about at this time of night?'

'You. Me.'

'Was it one of the girls? You knew where the black girl was tonight.'

'People here observe and steer clear.'

'Which someone, or more than one, would force him into a ruined house?' Edison said.

'As you mentioned, he's head of a firm. He's a target for some.'

'Which?'

'All sorts.'

'You think you know, don't you?'

Harpur went to get the flashlight from his car. When he returned, Whitehead left the Chrysler and joined him in a search of the deserted houses. Harpur might have preferred to work alone, but he sympathized with Edison's obvious need to show full commitment to Arlington, despite the deranged spells. Edison would wish to prove – prove especially to himself – that, if there'd been a fuck-up at the rendezvous spot, it didn't mean his commitment had slackened. The opposite: he'd been urgently trying to find Arlington safe elsewhere, say in a good interlude with Honorée.

They discovered nothing in the first two abandoned dwellings except fragments of window glass, mortar and brick debris, empty bottles and cans, some shrivelled, used condoms, squares of ancient matting, occasional shattered pieces of furniture, unrepairable and therefore not taken. Then they reached the third and final wreck on their schedule. Nothing on the ground floor. They climbed the stairs and opened the first door on to the landing.

'Oh, my caudillo, this is no place for you, alive or dead.'

Edison Whitehead spoke in a weak whisper. He was by Harpur's side, and gazed along the torch beam.

'At least two bullets in the head,' Harpur said, moving closer to Arlington's body.

Access to all the properties had been easy. They were boarded up, but time and kids and others had caused some of this protection to fall away. They had entered the first house through what would have been a kitchen window when intact. The last two had outer doors front or back that could be pushed open, the locks broken a long while ago. The boarding did have some use: although imperfect, it would help contain the sound of gunshots, and most probably smother it altogether if the gun had a silencer. Mike Arlington was lying on his back in a big, faded-pink, multi-chipped bath, his head and face a mess. There must be gaps in the slates just above. The bathroom's old-style plaster ceiling bulged downwards at two places, stained yellowy-brown, and dripped even now, a dry day and evening. Some plaster had fallen. The ceiling would tumble altogether soon. The floor was damp, and the bath under the smaller of the bulges had several inches of dark water in it, enough to half cover Arlington's legs and shoes and the back of his coat. Bits of plaster might be blocking the plughole. All taps, the towel rail and the lavatory seat had been pillaged, of course. If they ever decided to patch up these houses they'd have to get hold of someone in Neville's game to supply complete re-roofing stuff.

Edison said: 'Will the media need to be told how he was found – the bath and the filthy water? It's not dignified. This was a bathroom but is now a mockery of a bathroom. There's running water, but not from the plumbing. There's a bath with somebody in it, but it's not somebody it's some body, and some body fully dressed.'

Harpur made a pulse check on Arlington and found nothing. He called the Control Room. The Scene of Crime people would be here soon. He did a quick touchy-feely search without disturbing the body. 'His wallet, mobile phone, keys and comb are here, but he wasn't carrying a weapon,' he said.

'He's a businessman making business visits,' Edison said.

'Are *you* tooled up?'

'I was accompanying a businessman on business visits.'

Harpur called Iles. 'I'm driving,' Iles said, 'and not far away from Gladstone Square, as it happens, Col. I like to keep an eye on the Valencia.'

'Honorée is with a slate, tile and chimney brick old lad called Neville,' Harpur replied.

'Hers is a very democratic profession, Col,' Iles said.

He arrived at the house in five minutes, well before the Scene of Crime contingent. He brought a second torch. 'This is going to educate that fucker, Upton,' he said.

'In which respect, sir?' Harpur asked.

'You making the find, Col. Me here within minutes,' Iles said. 'On the ballness. Exemplary.'

'But you were only handy because you were looking for a shag,' Edison remarked.

One of the things about Iles was that he would take insulting talk from almost anyone, crook or colleague, and not go nuts, but give them a cogent answer. 'We don't have to tell Upton that, do we, Whitehead?' Iles said. 'You won't want the circumstances of this find spread all over the media, will you, your boss and gallant hero dumped and dunked in a tapless bath?'

'I've mentioned that to Mr Harpur,' Edison said.

'There you are, then,' Iles said. 'Some reciprocal silence would be in order, I think.'

'The Chief was down here this afternoon talking to Honorée,' Harpur said. 'Arlington did pix.'

'That poor kid. She needs someone to manage her diary,' Iles said. 'But we'll see changes now. Sir Matthew will realize he's wandering in the dark when he tries to understand the commodity trade here. He'll see he needs our help, Col. I'm ready to give him that help, despite his contrariness, and I'm sure you are, Harpur.'

Edison pointed to Arlington. Iles's torch threw a huge shadow of the gesture on one of the filthy bathroom walls. Edison said: 'But who did this?'

'That's one of those questions, isn't it?' Iles said. 'Arlington was with you, wasn't he – just the two of you at times? Are you carrying anything?'

'Mr Harpur has already asked me,' Edison said.

'He would. It's the obvious question,' Iles said. 'You wouldn't be the first bodyguard to see off his master.' He reached out with one hand and frisked Whitehead. 'Zilch.' Then he searched Arlington and brought out the wallet and mobile. He flipped through the wallet and replaced it. He put the phone in his pocket. 'Luckily, the water hasn't reached the front of his jacket. Quite dry. You won't mention this, either, will you, Edison? I don't want that poor sweet girl involved. It's bad enough for her having to go with a nonentity named Neville. Like you, I'll find this patch meaner and drabber without General Franco. Sir Matthew didn't take either to him or me. Well, Franco's gone now. I'll probably hang on a while, though.'

TWELVE

Margaret Ember hadn't been able to wait much longer at eleven Carteret Drive in the hope of seeing Karen Lister. Margaret had allowed herself half an hour, the half hour she'd snipped off the end of the fitness class. The visit was something she didn't want Ralph to know about, at least not yet. So, she'd set herself that maximum: pity it had to be taken up by Frank and Beryl only. If Karen had been there, Margaret would have asked her some delicate questions, such as whether she'd heard that inside the Shale firm Ralph was still considered responsible for the Jaguar deaths, and therefore also considered a target, plus, perhaps, his family. She continued to think of it as the Shale firm, even though Manse held only the formal post of chairman now. Ralph wouldn't be pleased if he knew she were seeking that kind of information from the other outfit, whatever its name today.

When she got back to Low Pastures, she found Ralph preparing to go to The Monty in Shield Terrace for his customary night stint. The children were watching television in what Ralph called 'the screening room'. All right, the room had a screen in it, but Margaret thought the name slightly big-time, slightly Ralph. Perhaps Charlton Heston had a screening room, where he could view films of himself as a hero. Margaret allowed Fay and Venetia another hour and then ordered them to bed.

After they'd gone, she and Ralph talked for a while about the class and its exertions.

Ralph liked to be at The Monty for the latter part of the evening to check takings, make sure the place was properly locked up, and put the money in his safe or take it to the out-of-hours bank depository. Tonight, as he was about to leave, he had a phone call on the landline. He listened for a minute and then said, 'There's *always* a crisis at the bloody Valencia.

A pain. Any more detail, let me know. I'll be at the club, thank God, on the other side of the city.'

'What is it?' Margaret said.

'Big police activity down there. Part of Gladstone Square cordoned off. Cars – marked and unmarked. An ambulance. And somebody must have rung TV. Cameras and lights, plus reporter.'

'What is it?'

'Not known at present. Or not known to the lad who phoned.'

'Which lad phoned?'

'One of our people working there.'

'Are you – we – involved?'

'How would we be?' he said.

'Why did he ring you, then?'

'He probably thinks I need to be briefed about what's happening on the territory.'

'And *do* you need it?' She thought he'd like the notion that any important incident in the city should be reported to him. *Shall we tell the President?* Yes. He saw himself as a fulcrum and a synthesizer. Sometimes she loved him for this egomania and his divine ability to keep it stoked up. Dear, wonderful, all-conquering Ralph. Sometimes she despised him for it: pathetic, posturing, screening-room Ralph. 'What kind of incident might it be?' she said.

'It's the Valencia. It could be anything – anything rough.'

'An ambulance, you said.'

'Probably routine turnout for an emergency call to one of those places.'

'Which places?'

'The big, old houses in Gladstone, some abandoned and decaying fast.'

'Why would anybody go into one of those?'

'It's the Valencia.'

'What does that mean, Ralph?'

'It has its own ways.'

'We all do.'

'The Valencia especially.'

She realized she was being told, without being told, not to ask too much. She'd been given her approved quota of what had been said on the phone, and that, in her husband's opinion, should be enough: police cars, an ambulance, police cordoning-tape. She needn't know any more than these symptoms, though *he* might. Ralph left for the club and she went to bed.

In the morning, before the school run, she switched on the local TV news in the screening room and watched the night scene at Gladstone Square. It was just as Ralph had described. The presenter spoke excitedly of 'considerable police activity' and said Assistant Chief Constable Desmond Iles and Detective Chief Superintendent Colin Harpur had been present, 'as well as scene of crime specialists and other officers, uniformed and plain clothed'. It was believed a body had been found on the first floor of one of the abandoned properties, but police had not yet completed an identification, nor disclosed who had discovered the body and reported it. 'Gladstone Square is in an area of the city known as the Valencia, after its main thoroughfare. It has a busy nightlife,' the commentator said. The media had to be tactful, but not opaque. 'Busy nightlife' was an acceptable, jolly sort of phrase, and the audience would hear 'drugs and tarts'.

Despite the Shale murders, Margaret almost always drove the children to school; a different private school from Laurent and Matilda Shale's, but involving about the same amount of travel. Ralph couldn't do it because he usually slept on a while in the mornings after his club duties. Someone from the firm always rode with Margaret and her daughters both ways and brought a variety of company vehicles for the trips, to make clue by car difficult. Margaret conscientiously changed routes to and from Bracken Collegiate every day. She supposed the escort had a gun, but didn't ask Ralph: it was one of those questions best kiboshed.

When she returned today, Ralph's Bentley had gone from the Low Pastures forecourt. Now and then he would cut short his sleep to attend to something special in one of the businesses. Today, the something special might have to do with those Gladstone Square events, though she knew he'd deny it. The bodyguard left, and he or another heavy from the firm would come back in the afternoon to pick up Fay and Venetia at Bracken with either herself or Ralph. It might have been simpler to allow one of Ralph's people to take and bring the children on his own, but neither of them fancied this idea. It would be to dodge out of a responsibility. It would be casual, and being casual could lead to casualties.

A little before midday she was in the kitchen when she heard the sound of an unfamiliar car engine approaching up the long drive, definitely not the Bentley. This troubled her, and she was surprised at how much it troubled her. Vehicles strange to her quite often came to Low Pastures on normal domestic calls – the postman or woman, shop delivery vans. Why should she get so tense today? She went quickly to the front of the house and stood hidden by the folds of a drawn-back curtain. She saw a grey Ford Focus almost at the forecourt. As far as she could make out there were two people in it, a woman driving, a man in the passenger seat, both elderly. They drew nearer and stopped near her Lexus. Now, she recognized Beryl and Frank, Karen Lister's neighbours from Carteret Drive.

They were people used to spying on others and so seemed to expect to be spied on here. That didn't mean they stared at the Low Pastures windows, trying to spot a watcher. But they put on a flattering little charade, aimed to please any onlooker in the property. They acted out what Margaret regarded as token awe at the sight of the house and gardens, gazing around in nicely equal spells, left, right, up to the roof and chimneys, down to the paddocks and terraces: a very capable performance.

She couldn't tell whether they'd seen her behind the curtain in the screening room, but reckoned it wouldn't matter whether they had or not. They'd suppose there would be eyes on them from somewhere and the show must continue. They had their established notion of what windows were for and assumed one or more of them in the Low Pastures frontage might now be operating as such: windows invited occupants to observe things and people outside. Beryl and Frank would automatically adjust their behaviour to suit. Margaret admired the phoney thoroughness of it. She could almost feel their put-on reverence for the place. And it deserved reverence, though not this cooked-up sort.

Why were they here? How did they trace her and find the house? She had not given them even her first name, and certainly no address.

Frank nodded at the Lexus parked near the front door and smiled. The bell rang, and she did her own bit of acting, too – delayed for three minutes before responding, as though she'd been in the back part of the house and unaware of the visitors' arrival, not having a nervy squint from behind drapes.

'You'll wonder what brings us to your fine home,' Beryl said.

'And magnificent setting,' Frank said.

There was a kind of rhythm to their statements. It reminded Margaret of Psalms learned at school: first, the main pronouncement, then an addition or adjustment – *the heavens declare the glory of God; and the firmament showeth his handiwork.*

'Oh, yes, the setting, too. Obviously,' Beryl said. 'The trees bordering the drive. A real autumn colour display, bright red, russet, evergreen.'

'It was something of a gamble, our coming here,' Frank said.

'A gamble?' Margaret said. She did her best to keep from her voice the irritation she felt, bordering on fury. This had replaced her apprehension. They talked in the porch so far. She wasn't ready to ask them in. She didn't want another duet about the distinction of the house – its interior now. Well, she didn't want these two in the house at all. For one thing, Ralph might return from wherever he'd gone. For another thing . . . for another thing she just didn't want them on the premises.

'We knew we had it right when we saw the Lexus,' Frank said. 'Distinctive.' He wore a Barbour jacket, perhaps put on to come into the country and visit a manor house.

'We looked in on Karen this morning and told her that you'd called but couldn't wait any longer,' Beryl said. 'She was very curious and mystified. Of course, we had no name, and she asked us to describe you. I think we must have done it quite well because almost at once she said, "It sounds like Margaret Ember." I mentioned the red Lexus and she exclaimed, "Yes! Margaret Ember from Low Pastures. Her husband is in business and runs The Monty club. But what did she want? Do you know? Margaret Ember turned up here? Really?" That's more or less what she said, isn't it, Frank? I definitely remember that "really". It showed true surprise at such an occurrence.'

'Yes, indeed,' Frank said. 'Extremely curious and mystified.'

Beryl said: 'We didn't mention that we'd seen her leave the house just after that visitor – the maybe police detective—'

'The fair-haired Rocky Marciano almost-look-alike,' Frank said. 'Perhaps Harpur.'

'—and seem to follow him,' Beryl said. 'That might have sounded as if we were snooping on her.'

'Yes, I suppose it might,' Margaret said.

'It's this detective – the possibly Colin Harpur – that we'd like to discuss with you, Mrs Ember,' Frank said.

Margaret had a sudden notion, an instinct, that the two might, after all, have something worth listening to. She said: 'But we shouldn't be talking out here. Please, do come in. What can I have been thinking of?' She'd been thinking of how to get rid of them without blatant rudeness. Now, she amended that.

'Thanks so much,' Beryl said.

'Such a wonderful hall,' Frank said, gazing. 'Spacious and yet welcoming, even cosy. One can imagine long ago the squire returning gratefully to a hall like this after an arduous day's hunting.'

'The exposed stone – so authentic,' Beryl said. 'Quite a difference from plasterboard! Oh, yes, plasterboard is smoother and easier to hang wallpaper on, but this is a building obviously built to last, proud of its rugged, genuine materials.'

Margaret took them into the drawing room. It had views over the paddocks and fields to the sea. She went to the kitchen and put the kettle on.

When she came back, Frank said: 'Yes, this police

officer – the possible Detective Chief Superintendent Harpur –
interests Beryl and me.'

'You know him?' Margaret asked.

'Have you seen the local TV news this morning?' Frank
replied. He seemed to have taken over from Beryl the main
role in their chat team. The way he ignored Margaret's
question and went on to one of his own got close to
being autocratic, despite that feeble moustache and sad, old
stoop.

'I did glance at the news,' Margaret said.

'Some kind of crisis in the Valencia,' Frank said. 'Gladstone
Square.'

'Yes, I think I remember. An area cordoned off,' Margaret
said. 'A lot of cars. A large Chrysler? An ambulance.'

'A lot of cars, yes,' he replied.

'Frank thinks one of them rather significant,' Beryl said.
'He's not good on motors and their make, but he did notice
the Chrysler and another.' She had on a brown car coat of
high-grade leather over an amber blouse and tan corduroy
trousers.

'I'd like you, if you would, Mrs Ember, to think back to
our conversation over the front fence in Carteret Drive last
evening,' Frank said. He sounded now like a QC, lulling a
witness before the cross-examination onslaught started. Frank
could have made good use of a courtroom wig.

'How small and architecturally insignificant those houses
seem against this one,' Beryl said. 'Yet it suits us. What would
we be doing with paddocks at our age, I wonder?'

'I happened to look along the street as we talked then, if
you recall,' Frank said.

'Observant. Frank is like that. He seeks the full picture,'
Beryl said. 'The context, if, in fact, that full picture, that
context, is available. They're not always, of course, but
fragments placed together – skilfully placed together –
inspirationally placed together, in fact – can sometimes add
up to such a picture, as might be so in this case. Frank
refuses to blow his own trumpet so, occasionally, I will blow
it for him.' She put a hand up to her lips for a moment as
though she'd spotted a double entendre here and wanted to

push the words back, particularly the word 'blow', most probably.

'A black car – a Mazda you said, Mrs Ember – was parked some way from where we talked, facing in our direction and, at first, I thought it empty. My eyes are not what they were, you know,' Frank said.

'There might not have been much significance to it were that so,' Beryl said.

'What significance *was* there?' Margaret replied. 'An unoccupied parked car. There are always plenty in the street, especially at night.'

'But *was* it empty, you see?' Beryl said.

'Ah,' Margaret said. Of course, she'd noticed Frank had said that 'at first' he'd thought the Mazda empty. Stand by for a revision. She accepted a kind of duty, though, to play half stupid, so they would feel superior, keen to correct her by getting on with the tale.

'Frank was describing his original impression,' Beryl said.

They intended to roll out the story in their own style – place together those 'fragments' Beryl had spoken of, and do it at their chosen pace, which was not hell-for-leather. Margaret realized they aimed to intrigue her, make her desperate to hear what they knew, subordinate her to their insights, because she lived in a gorgeous house with authentic bare stone walls, as against their smaller and very average one held together by plasterboard.

She went back to the kitchen and made tea. She returned with a tray and mugs, not china cups, which might have looked chichi, or, worse than that, middle-class. She put the tray on the rosewood table. Beryl was sitting on the blue, loose-covered chesterfield. Frank had an armchair near the Regency sideboard. Margaret took another armchair opposite him.

Frank said: 'You mentioned a Chrysler in the TV footage of the Gladstone Square incident. I'd agree. There *was* a Chrysler. Yes, one of the big models. Even I could recognize a Chrysler.'

'"A Chrysler trying to look like a Bentley." This was Frank's comment when he saw it on the film. It sort of *punctured* the car's pretensions, as it were,' Beryl said. 'Frank loathes grandiosity.'

Margaret didn't mention that her husband might turn up soon in a Bentley that *was* a Bentley. Did that amount to grandiosity? She'd like to get them back into their Focus and fucked off before Ralph appeared and didn't want to provoke extra chat about car makes. In any case, a reference to Ralph's sublime limo might be the equivalent of the good china: blatant swank.

'But a little behind the Chrysler?' Frank asked gently.

'Don't remember,' Margaret said. That was true. There'd been a lot of vehicles. She realized now, though, that the Mazda must have been there. The particles of Frank's and Beryl's yarn were about to add up to something. She couldn't tell what.

'A black Mazda,' Frank declared.

'Honestly?' Margaret exclaimed, making sure the word reeked of astonishment.

Beryl said: 'We both noted it, in fact, and we cried out the words themselves, "A black Mazda!" to guarantee the other noticed it, which, clearly, was unnecessary, since we jointly observed the vehicle standing there and – also jointly – appreciated its significance.'

'What significance did you think it had, jointly?' Margaret said.

'I would like to take you back again to previous events in Carteret Drive,' My Learned Friend Frank said. 'I'll reach in due course another relevant mention of the Mazda. But sequence is important – a saga properly managed.'

'Frank has always striven for that kind of orderliness and clarity in describing a pattern of events,' Beryl said. 'It's very much him.'

'Mrs Ember, you left Carteret Drive when there continued to be no answer at number eleven,' Frank said. 'Shortly afterwards, Jason returned in the estate car with the same friends – at least, the same as far as one could tell, under the street lights – not very bright – and in the brief pause they made while Jason got out of the vehicle. He appeared to give a thumbs-up gesture. Presumably they'd had a pleasant evening somewhere.'

'Thumbs up?' Margaret said.

'To the pair in the Volvo,' Beryl said.

'It could have been a "thank you" for the lift home, or a signal that they'd successfully pulled off something – achieved something – or simply an acknowledgement that they'd had that pleasant evening together.'

'Achieved what?' Margaret said.

'Well, obviously Frank can't answer that, can he?' Beryl said. There was no sharpness in her tone, just a mild, patient reasonableness.

Margaret would agree her question had been absurd. Frank wasn't clairvoyant, merely a grade-A neighbourhood watcher. Margaret would have to go on wondering about the thumbs up, suspecting about the thumbs up, disliking the thumbs up.

'Number eleven had remained in darkness until Jason arrived. Now, there were lights on downstairs,' Beryl said.

'And then, fortunately, we were in the front room again when Karen's Mini appeared,' Frank said. 'She found parking a little way up the street and came back on foot to the house – came back running to the house, and I mean *really* running, an undoubted sprint, although in heels. Joy – that's what showed in her face, despite the exertion – joy, considerable excitement, relief.'

'Relief at what?' Margaret said.

'Now, Mrs Ember, you may well ask what has happened to the black Mazda in our account of things,' Frank replied.

'Yes,' Margaret said.

'I've said I thought the car looked empty when I noticed it during our conversation over the front fence,' Frank said, 'although I had an unexplainable inkling that it might contain somebody.'

'Now and then, or even oftener, Frank does have inklings,' Beryl said. 'How, then, do we define "inklings" – i.e., what *is* an inkling, especially the kind of inkling Frank has? A strange word, isn't it? Strange, yet seeming to contain within itself – that is, within its sound when spoken – yes, seeming to contain its own meaning. Doesn't it suggest something insubstantial, even slight – perhaps because it rhymes with "tinkling" – insubstantial even slight, but of a subtle, unexplainable, undeniable power?'

Shut your gob and let Frank get on with his dissertation, you tinkling old cow. 'Fascinating,' Margaret replied.

'Suddenly, this inkling became something else,' Frank said.

'It's the way inklings occasionally will – inklings generally, not just Frank's,' Beryl explained.

'A little while after Karen returned at such a gallop to their house, the Mazda moved off,' Frank said.

'Had you seen anyone go to it?' Margaret said.

'Not in the sense that you probably mean,' Frank said. 'Nobody had come out from one of the houses and climbed in.'

'So the inkling had been a correct inkling, although insubstantial?' Margaret asked. 'There had been someone in the car?'

'This will really shock you, Mrs Ember,' Beryl said.

'Yes, there *had* been someone in the car,' Frank said. 'But in the back.'

'This would account for Frank's uncertainty,' Beryl said.

'Now, obviously, the Mazda couldn't be driven away by someone sitting in the back,' Frank said.

'Hardly!' Beryl had a merry laugh.

'The off-side rear door opened, a man got out and then re-entered the car, but taking the driving seat now. He drove out of Carteret,' Frank said.

'We're speculating that police detectives are trained to occupy the rear of a car when it's being used for secret surveillance,' Beryl said. 'This would make them much less visible than when behind the wheel or in the front passenger seat, especially as headrests obscure the rear of the saloon.'

'The disadvantage comes, of course, when the detective wants to drive off and has to get out and change seats,' Frank said.

'You believe this detective was Harpur and that he drove to the Valencia, parked in Gladstone Square, and the TV camera showed the vehicle there?' Margaret asked.

'The build and overall appearance of the man makes Frank think it was Harpur,' Beryl said.

'Which suggests a link between Jason and/or Karen and whatever it is that happened in that abandoned house – possibly the finding of a body, according to the telly news,' Margaret said.

'We felt it was something you should know about, since you were at number eleven last night seeking Karen – possibly have a friendship with her,' Beryl said.

'No, not exactly that,' Margaret said.

'Whatever,' Beryl replied.

'I hope you didn't mind our bursting in on you,' Frank said.

'I'm grateful,' Margaret said. She felt guilty at having been so resentful earlier. The information they brought – the laboriously, cleverly, joined-up 'fragments' – could be important for her. She couldn't tell what they meant, and Frank and Beryl might not know either. But they meant *something*, and something serious. Margaret decided she wouldn't be calling at number eleven Carteret Drive to quiz Karen about feelings in the Shale camp. That mission seemed naive, almost simple-minded, to her now. There were all kinds of involvements and shadowy connections. She was afraid of blundering about in a scene she knew only a fraction of. Perhaps that early tension was her body intuiting a threat.

Frank said: 'But I think you'll understand, Mrs Ember, that we have also a selfish interest in calling on you.'

Margaret felt a sudden marked reversal in the nature of this meeting. These two had seemed tentative and gabby. She'd considered herself in command of the situation, able to shape it and, perhaps, profit from it. But a kind of upending seemed under way. Frank's tone had sharpened. So had Beryl's. Had they pre-choreographed this interview? Were they much smarter than Margaret had thought? 'Selfish?' she said.

'We considered it should be face-to-face,' Beryl said. 'This is not something for the telephone, even if we had a number, which we don't, since you seem to be ex-directory.'

'Our point is this, Mrs Ember: we apparently live next door to people in whom a highly placed police officer has a considerable, though clandestine, interest,' Frank said. 'Rather worrying. You spoke of a link between our neighbours and the unusual situation overnight in Gladstone Square at the Valencia, a link via this watchful police officer and his Mazda car. Mrs Ember, everyone who lives in this city has an idea of the main business that goes on in the Valencia. Or possibly I should say businesses. But the principal one is the pushing of drugs, isn't it?'

'This is commonplace in most inner city areas,' Beryl said.

'Possibly it is unique to our city that this selling is to some degree tolerated by the police,' Frank said. 'Most local people have heard of this, also. We have grandchildren at school who mention it.'

'And they mention, also, the names of some of the most significant people in this regime – on the one hand the Assistant Chief Constable, Desmond Iles, and on the other – on, that is, the trading side – the two firms, Shale and, yes, Ember,' Beryl said.

'You will see why we are curious and somewhat anxious about your visit to our neighbourhood last evening,' Frank said.

'As we've mentioned, we are very fond of Karen and have never had any cause to think ill of her, nor, indeed, of Jason,' Beryl said. 'Now, though, we are bound to be conscious of new factors.'

'Which?' Margaret replied. She knew which, of course, and realized that pretending not to would look ludicrous. But she needed Beryl and Frank to do the talking for a while longer. She wanted time to adjust to the changed state of things.

'One new factor is that linkage between our neighbours and some kind of crisis at the Valencia, the Valencia being what it is,' Frank said. 'And – excuse me, Mrs Ember, but this has to be said—'

'Can't be avoided,' Beryl said.

'Perhaps the most striking development,' Frank said, 'is the visit to our next doors by someone from one of the two families notable in the local substances trade.'

'Dominant in that trade,' Beryl said.

'Dominant,' Frank replied.

'Naturally, we, like most other people in this city, are aware that following the retirement of Mr Mansel Shale from hands-on control of his companies, a new precariousness has come upon the drugs trade.'

'This is a word – "precariousness", "precarious" – that Frank has frequently used about present conditions in the commerce here, and I believe it justified,' Beryl said. 'There is bound to be a jockeying to replace him. Oh, I've heard – again from the grandchildren – that Mansel Shale named a successor. But, apparently, this successor, while very talented in some respects, also has massive flaws.'

'What we are getting at, Mrs Ember, is that we've entered a time of acute instability in the business set-up, and this could lead to what are known as "turf wars", in which individuals or gangs try to take over ground previously secured by a powerful and skilled leader, but now – as they see it – sloppily run and conquerable.'

'There's a saying, "Nature abhors a vacuum",' Beryl said. 'Always, we'll find forces attempting to fill that vacuum, and attempting it with extreme ruthlessness and disregard for the interests of those who might be accidentally, innocently, involved.'

'I'm sure you can see the direction of our thinking,' Frank said. 'And the reason for our uneasiness. Well, more than uneasiness. For our fears.'

'No, I don't think I follow,' Margaret said, following.

'There is, first, the general feeling that we have become sucked into something rather questionable. We are friendly with Karen and to a lesser extent with Jason,' Beryl said. 'But now we have cause to think they might have a side to their lives which is . . . which is, well . . . dubious. And then – forgive the bluntness – we find we have been talking to you in a very public way when you called on one of these neighbours, to what purpose we, of course, cannot know. But as much about it as we *do* know is rather uncomfortable.'

'As if a situation – a rather mysterious and disturbing situation – has suddenly enveloped us,' Frank said.

'I don't know whether there is a "situation" or not, but even if there is, you're not part of it,' Margaret said.

'To be more specific: a very senior detective is apparently interested in our next-door neighbour, or neighbours,' Frank said. 'This detective is also concerned with some kind of crisis in a drug-dealing area of the city. One of our neighbours is visited, unsuccessfully at this stage, by the wife of a so-called drugs "baron". Surely the pile up of these elements would make almost anyone worried. We have heard of drive-by attacks during gang battles in other cities. Not all such onslaughts are totally accurate. Bullets are sprayed. Do we live next to someone who might be a target for one of these fusillades? I don't think anxiety about such dangers is alarmist or cowardly. We might be hit, though in our own property.'

Especially if you were having a pry from the front room. But Margaret said: 'This is all *so* speculative.'

'It is the wider sense of being implicated and helpless to resist that troubles us,' Frank said.

'Is your family firm, your husband, in some kind of alliance with Jason?' Beryl replied. 'Was that why you called at the house? We don't want to be drawn into anything potentially violent, you see,' Beryl said. 'At our age.'

'We felt it best to be open with you about these concerns,' Frank said.

Margaret longed to turn full-power ratty and tell them to get out of the house. Their intrusiveness, their yellowness, their insolence – renamed by them 'bluntness' and 'openness' – and their nosiness all angered her. She knew they ought to have done more than that: they ought to have enraged her, as they would enrage Ralph if he came back and heard their bleating. But she couldn't get beyond a fairly mild resentment. After all, in describing their own feelings they had described fairly accurately some of hers. She, too, feared getting sucked into a scene which she didn't properly understand and certainly couldn't control. The reason she'd been at number eleven Carteret Drive was to see whether Karen Lister could help her understand and possibly control – part control, anyway – the life that Ralph's position in the drugs baronage imposed on her, and, possibly, on the children. Margaret shared that sense of being 'enveloped', not suddenly in her case, but relentlessly and totally.

'No,' Margaret said, 'my husband has no alliance with Jason Wensley. I'm sure you'll be safe. I don't think I'll be visiting their house again.'

'But why were you there last evening?' Beryl said.

'And now I must go out to an appointment,' Margaret said, standing. Maybe that word, 'appointment', sounded woolly and pompous on its own, so she added something to give it exactness and ordinariness. 'A dental appointment. It's been good to talk with you both again.'

'Oh dear, have we overstayed?' Frank said. He and Beryl also stood.

'Not at all. But I must make a move,' Margaret said. She thought she'd drive around for half an hour going nowhere special, then come home.

She did that and when she returned found Ralph there. He seemed cheery. 'Manse rang while you were out,' he said. 'He wanted a meeting, one to one over at his place straight away.'

Shale lived in a big, old ex-rectory on the edge of the city. 'Is he all right?' she said.

'Still in grief, but not totally floored any longer.'

'Poor, poor Manse.'

'His attitude has changed.'

'Which?'

'Towards me. Towards our firm.'

'Changed in a good way? I mean, if he rang and asked for the meeting.' She felt grand relief, not full scale yet, still uncertain and tentative, but a start.

'Yes, a good way,' Ralph said. 'What would you call a good way, Maggie?'

He doesn't think, after all, that you laid on the Jaguar kill-ings, and so won't be looking for how to get square. She didn't say this, though. 'Well, friendlier, I suppose.'

'Yes, friendlier.' He had a chuckle about this, obviously finding it a jolly slice of understatement. The scar along his jawline, so fascinating to some women, seemed to take on an unflickering, carmine glow from his amusement. 'He doesn't suspect any longer that I sent the gunman who got his wife and son by mistake, intending to wipe out him.'

'Did he ever believe that, for heaven's sake?' Margaret replied, knowing Shale probably did. And half believing it, or more, herself.

'The boy was a mistake, but she wasn't.'

That shocked Margaret. It took a while for her to reply. 'Someone wanted Naomi Shale murdered?' Margaret said. 'Is that really so, Ralph?'

'There seem to have been people in London she'd offended.'

'And they sent someone to kill her – is that what you're saying? Is it credible? What *sort* of people did she know in London? I thought she was some kind of journalist.'

'Journalists get killed, and not just when they're covering wars.'

'For what, though, in Naomi's case?'

'The boy got hit because he was there and didn't keep down in the back of the car. Naomi was hit because people wanted her dead.'

'Which people?'

'She and Manse met in London, at an art gallery, you know. He's a Pre-Raphaelite man. She was connected with a celebrity paper – part-owned it at the time, I think. It did – still does, maybe – interviews with big names visiting the capital, puffing their shows or books or romances. That kind of thing. It put her in touch with a lot of wealthy types. Some of them had a very expensive habit. She could what's called "facilitate".'

'Put them in touch with suppliers?'

'That kind of thing. This was a dangerous area. One supplier might get pissed off because she'd pushed one of her clients towards another supplier. These people can be unforgiving.'

'And Manse has only just found out about this aspect of her life?'

'He had a hint or two just after the killings, apparently, but ignored them. He didn't want to think of her like that. Protective of her memory. Recently, though, a couple more bits of evidence have come to him, and he can't dismiss them. He wouldn't say what they are, but they're enough to alter his mind.'

'Wonderful,' Margaret said. 'Well, wonderful in a way. Wonderful for you. And for me. Not for Manse.'

He gave her a bit of a gaze. 'Did you think I'd set up the slaughter, then?'

I wasn't sure. But she didn't say this, either. 'Of course not. But it's wonderful that Manse can accept this at last.'

'Has to accept it. What he's heard about her and her contacts up there lately is cast iron, apparently, irrefutable.'

'Someone punishing Naomi?'

'That sort of thing. He's able to feel less guilt about it.'

'Guilt?'

'He thought he'd brought the attack on her because she was mistaken for him, but also because she was associated with him and his firm. That self-blame has lifted. He's re-emerging. He'd like to go back to the old arrangement here – the two firms working peacefully alongside each other.'

'He'll take over the running of his company again?'

'It sickens him to see the way things have gone. The body found in that Valencia house is one of his people, possibly killed by someone wanting the leadership. Manse sees a kind of chaos and waste. He has to return.'

'And *can* the old arrangement be resumed? What about the new Chief? Isn't he against tolerance – against the Iles policy? He sent that gang to search the house, didn't he?'

'Which resulted in nothing, in a fiasco. Of course it did. There was nothing to find.'

'Did you get a warning, though, that it was coming?'

'I'm sent intimations from their side sometimes.'

'Who supplies them? Who exactly?'

'Manse and I think Iles can turn Upton towards sense,' Ralph replied. 'He'll convince the Chief that Nature abhors a vacuum, and for reasons which have just become obvious. Shale back at work will fill that emptiness, make peace possible again. And I bet Iles has looked into Upton's life and background and found something he can use to pressure him.'

'Many would find Iles a disgrace.'

'Many would. Many do.' Ralph put an arm around her shoulders, as he had the other day. She liked it better now, though. 'There were times lately when I thought you might take the kids and run again,' he said.

She put her own arm around him. 'That's crazy. Once is enough.'

'Once is too many.'

THIRTEEN

Harpur knew that the Assistant Chief's smart skill at charting other people's motives came as part of a more general, brilliant flair in measuring up character. Iles did some measuring up now and, as ever, had it totally right. For once, though, he was too late. He said: 'I worry about what this will do to Edison Whitehead, Col.'

'It's bad,' Harpur said. 'And there's similar stuff on radio and TV news.'

'Who gabbed?' Iles said. '"Sources" are mentioned here. Which fucking sources?' They were in his office. He wore uniform and looked very commanding but edgy. He had the local morning paper on the desk in front of him.

'Could be paramedics from the ambulance. And there was a doctor, eventually,' Harpur said.

Iles read from the paper. '"The body has been identified as that of Michael Redvers Arlington, aged thirty-one, of Peel Street, Lakeside. Sources say he had been shot twice in the face and was found fully clothed in a pink bath on the first floor of one of the abandoned Victorian properties in Gladstone Square, off Valencia Esplanade. Several inches of rain had accumulated in the bath from gaps in the roof, the drainage outlet and pipe having become clogged with fallen plaster. Sources believe the body had been placed in the bath as some kind of macabre joke, the still-preserved, bright-pinkness of the bath – despite vandalism and wear – contrasting strongly with the dark murkiness of the collected water. Mr Arlington is believed to have had connections with the drug trading that takes place in the district known as the Valencia, and had recently assumed hands-on leadership of one of the major firms."

'It's the mention of the bath's pinkness, Col – double mention – the jammed plughole, and the filthy water that will distress Edison. Pink is a sneer. If the bath had been white and had some still-preserved bright whiteness, despite vandalism and wear, somehow it wouldn't be so demeaning for his champ.'

For his caudillo. But Harpur didn't tell the ACC that in Whitehead's initial shock and agony at first seeing the body he had for a moment embraced Arlington's extensive, daft, fascist fantasy. To feed Iles this clinching detail would be an insult to the ACC. He had no need of any extra pointer to the state of Edison's soul. Iles's short conversation with him near the pink bath, plus the Assistant Chief's sharp instincts, told him enough.

Iles stood and checked his appearance in the long cheval mirror. He took his cap from a peg. 'We should go to him, Col.'

'Both of us?'

'This is not something to skimp on, Harpur. He'll blame himself for General Franco's death. Edison is the sort. He failed in his duty to protect.'

'I've told him it wasn't his fault. Arlington went off alone on a big, mock-up African march in the Valencia.'

'You won't have satisfied Edison. He'll convict himself of slackness. There's a kind of nobility in him. I sensed it at once in the bathroom.' Iles began to tremble and shout-scream and wave both hands around, using a finger on each of them, turn and turn about, to point at Harpur. 'Nobility is not a quality I see in you, Harpur, nor in anyone who . . .'

'I'll find Edison's address in his dossier, sir.' Harpur got the finger from Iles doubled every time, once actual, once in the mirror, where the left became the right and vice versa. It seemed an attack from a multitude of directions.

'. . . nor in anyone who targets another man's wife, with no regard for . . .'

'And then I'll bring the Mazda.'

'. . . no regard for normal decency or for the respect and fealty due from you to a superior officer. That's what I mean when I refer to Edison's noble nature. He can't bear to think he betrayed General Franco. And you – were you ever conscious of having betrayed me?'

Harpur drove.

Iles said: 'Put the screamer on.'

Harpur activated the siren and the flashing blue lights on

top of the dashboard. He took the speed up to seventy. 'They'll see us on the Control Room screens and wonder what it's about. The Chief will be told.'

'There are many things about the Chief I admire, Col.'

'Which?'

'Oh, yes, many.'

The bath in Edison Whitehead's red-brick town-house, also at Lakeside, was white, and had not been knocked about by vandals or wear. The dossier said he lived alone after a split from his partner, Graham Lee-Tremayne, a year ago. Iles and Harpur couldn't get any answer when Iles rang the bell. Harpur had some good keys with him and opened the door. Iles called Edison's name in a coaxing, pacifying, very unfrightening tone. After that, the house stayed quiet.

Harpur said: 'Someone might have phoned him about the newspaper reports and he's gone to get a copy in the supermarket.'

'Yes, someone might,' Iles said, 'but we'd better look in the bathroom, I think, don't you, Harpur?'

They went upstairs, Iles calling out Edison's name again, softly. He was in the bath, wearing quite a decent suit and a blue tie with silver stripes. The bath contained about the same amount of water as Arlington had been sitting in at Gladstone Square. This water was red, though. There was blood on the lino-covered floor. One of his arms hung out of the bath, a vein or artery severed. His other arm and hand were in the water, probably with the same sort of damage.

'He's seen *Godfather Two*,' Iles said. 'Franky the fink does himself like that. It's how the Romans used to take themselves off if things got too tough. I told you Edison had a noble core.'

Harpur often heard about the *Godfather* and even the God*mother* from his daughters. Now Iles.

The ACC reached into the water and recovered a sizeable kitchen knife. They had closed the front door. The bell rang twice. Harpur went downstairs to open up. Mansel Shale stood on the doorstep, staring past Harpur and up the stairs at Iles, who had the knife in his right hand. 'Manse!' Iles called. 'You've been reading the papers, watching the telly, have you?'

'I had to come round,' Manse said. 'I knew Edison would be quite upset.'

'Well, yes,' Iles said.

Harpur stood to one side, and Shale came in and climbed the stairs. He had on a pinstripe, lawyerly suit of superb but old cloth and cut. Manse was known to buy traditional gear from Oxfam because for him they radiated class and history. Iles stood to one side, also, so Manse could enter the bathroom. Iles held the knife pointing downwards at his side and dripping mostly water.

'This sort of thing hardly ever happened when you were running your outfit, Manse,' Iles said. 'I mean really running it, not just figure-heading. I know I would have remembered if we'd had two deads in different baths on succeeding days. Col, do you recall anything like that when Manse had the reins?'

'I took Matilda to school and then came straight here,' Shale replied.

'In the Jaguar?' Iles said.

'I've been thinking of taking over again myself,' Shale said. 'It's terrible to see a firm falling to pieces like this.'

'Nature abhors a vacuum,' Iles said. He sat down on the side of the bath at the feet end of Edison. 'Someone else might want to grab the power. Well, someone else might have seen off Arlington.'

'My mother used to say, "A word is enough for the wise,"' Shale said.

'Mothers can come out with all sorts of stuff, can't they, Manse?' Iles said.

'I'll have a word if necessary.'

'With, say, Jason Ivan Claud Wensley?' Iles asked.

'That kind of thing, yes,' Shale said. 'I think he'll see my way is best.'

'He has chums,' Harpur said.

'They'll see it, too,' Shale said.

Upton called a mini-conference that afternoon. In the corridor, on their way to it, Iles said: 'I don't think I'll need the camera material, Col. It would degrade me.'

'Degrade you how?'

'This would be an Assistant Chief more or less putting the blackmail screws on a Chief.'

'Yes.'

'And it would be based on a misreading of what he was up to. He only wanted to quiz Honorée, not hire her. It would be unfair to him. Also, I wouldn't want it suggested anywhere that he'd moved in on a girl of mine.'

'She's not yours. She was with Neville last time I saw her.'

'That's different from Sir Matthew.'

'How?'

'You're not one for fine points, Harpur. "Decorum" is a mystery word to you.'

'He wanted to quiz her so as to damage you.'

'But he's the Chief, Harpur. That's what Chiefs are like – what helps *make* them Chiefs.'

The three of them sat in armchairs in Upton's suite. He said: 'Perhaps we've been going at this thing too fast, too head-on.'

'Excuse me, which thing, sir?' Iles inquired.

'The substances trade. These deaths – Arlington, now Whitehead. I didn't expect that sort of result.'

'Very unfortunate,' Iles said.

'And nothing came of the Low Pastures search,' Upton said.

'No, sir,' Harpur said.

'Perhaps there's something to be gained from a more gradual approach,' Upton said, 'though with the same ultimate aim.'

'It's odd, sir, but Col Harpur and I were just saying the same on our way here.'

'Yes, I expect so,' Upton said.

In the evening, Karen Lister called at Harpur's house. His vision of her dead face with the teeth on show was a mistake, then. There'd been two deaths, but neither hers: Franco and Edison instead. Jill opened the door when Karen rang. She wouldn't come in, though, but spoke on the doorstep once Harpur appeared in the hall to greet her. He sent Jill back into the living room and closed that door.

'What's going to happen to Jason?' she said.

'We're looking at a whole lot of angles,' Harpur said.

'Yes, but what will happen to him?'

'We're looking at a whole lot of angles,' Harpur said.

She turned and walked fast away.

When Harpur returned to the living room, Jill said: 'Is she going to be calling at the house often? Denise might have been here, you know. She said she'll come at about half past seven.'

'Yes, I do know,' Harpur said. 'Great.'